Cold Nights
A Deliver Us from Evil Erotica

B.G. Hing as Leah Hantel

Leah Hantel

Cold Nights © 2021 B.G. Hing

Cover Art by:

To the girls who fight.

Cold Nights

Chapter One

WE MET IN SECRET under the starry sky—bare feet in the sand, the moon, and Bloodstar overhead.

"Lenora," He crooned my name, and I felt butterflies in my stomach, a slosh of pleasant warmth in my pelvis, and my knees were weak. "Lenora, what are you doing out here in the middle of the night? Papa would have a fit!" He teased, knowing full well that I was out here, standing along the beachside of our wonderful city because of him. Because of his blond curls and his warm eyes, I had risked my parent's ire.

I held my breath when I spoke, "Lukas, don't tease me. I'm very nervous, you know."

His strong hands reached out and grabbed my shoulders. He pulled me, stumbling feet and all, towards him.

"There's no reason for you to be nervous, Lenora, my little sister. We are just out here for a nighttime stroll." He insisted, but I knew otherwise. I huffed at his words and pulled away from his grasp.

"Stop it, Lukas. Why do you like calling me your sister so much?"

This time he grabbed my chin instead, tilting my face up to his. He was gorgeous—a picture of youth and beauty. Strong chin, muscular arms. He made my heart swoon, even though it shouldn't have. My parents adopted him three years ago so that they could conserve his inheritance until he was old enough to claim it on his own. That made him my brother, and I knew it was wrong to have feelings like these, incredible deep feelings that stirred my body and soul.

And I couldn't help it.

Lukas leaned forward, down to my short self. I wasn't nearly as beautiful as him. My hair was a dusty brown, and my skin was thankfully clear from blemishes even though just a few years ago, I was plagued by adolescent pox that left a clear waving texture across my cheeks no matter how many creams I used. My heart thumped loudly in my chest. He was getting closer and closer, and I daringly imagined what it would be like to kiss him.

"I call you my sister so that I might be reminded that it's illegal to want this." His fingers brushed over my lips, increasing my heart's desperate fluttering. "You know, Lenora, I don't think it's working."

This was the moment! I was sure of it. I was sure his lips were going to touch mine, and I would be kissed by a man

I lusted after, a man I couldn't have. I thought my heart was going to give up from its frenetic pace and leave me weightless in the sand.

But that didn't happen at all.

From the houseline, back where our shared home was, I could hear my Papa call out.

"Lenora! *Lenora!*"

"Ah, maybe another time." Lukas grumbled and then raised his voice to meet our Papa's, "Over here! She was sleepwalking again! I caught her before she got in the ocean!"

His hand clasped on my disappointed arm and pulled me back to the house. There stood my Papa and Mama and our older brother, Jonathan. Thankfully my younger brother was still asleep inside. The three of them looked worried, and I'm sure they were. I did have a penchant for sleepwalking.

"Oh, thank God you caught her, Lukas," my Mama said and then embraced me as if I was a child. I wasn't, but Mama worried as if I was.

"Sorry I didn't bring her back sooner. I was trying to get her to wake up, so she didn't wander again." Lukas managed to sound decently apologetic, and there was no doubt my parents would buy his story. My older brothers were upstanding men, good for our community, and trustworthy. I did not doubt that my parents didn't have a single thought in their head that Lukas might have asked me down on the beach.

That he would have kissed me if we weren't interrupted, that maybe he would make love to me and fulfill my secret desires under the starlit sky.

"It's alright, Lukas, we know she's a wanderer." my Papa said before giving me a cursory glance. "I might have to bolt your door shut at night. There are too many bad things that can happen to a young woman like you on the beach."

I flushed with embarrassment and bowed my head.

"I'm sorry, Papa." My words probably were heard by the head of our household, but it was my Mama who responded.

"Oh, Lenora, it's not your fault." Her loving arms reached out to me, embracing me tight even though I had long been taller than her. "I'll sleep with you the rest of the night, just in case you start walking in your sleep again." She patted my shoulder lovingly, and I knew I would never be judged by her, not for imaginary sleepwalking anyway.

"Ok." I agreed meekly, still a little disappointed that the night hadn't gone differently. I glanced at Lukas, but he wasn't looking in my direction. He was yawning, stretching his arms over his head, and joking with Jonathan about something. I didn't pay much attention to what it was. I just let my Mama lead me back into our house, the whitewashed, sea sprayed building I had lived in from the day I was born. It only had one large floor; houseplants lined our hallways. My room was on the side of the house overlooking the sea. I had big windows where I could look down to the beachside and imagine what it would have been like if Lukas kissed me in the sand.

Instead, my hands rested on the window sill, and I sighed, looking into the sky. Almost a full moon and right by its side, the Bloodstar glowed a comforting crimson. Silently I wished to the heavens that I would soon feel my first kiss granted by the man I loved. *It can't be helped that Papa adopted him. That doesn't dissolve my feelings.*

"Come to bed, Lenora," Mama called, and I left the window and my silent prayers for love. I curled up and let Mama hold me while she fell asleep, and when I finally joined her, it was to dream of Lukas holding me.

Chapter Two

PEELING SWEET POTATOES WAS one of my least favorite jobs, but today was bread-making day, and Mama always sweetened the loaves with purple sweets. I sighed heavily, slicing off the rough skin with the best kitchen knife we had. I couldn't stop thinking about the other night. How close Lukas and I came to kissing. A first kiss, a kiss for the woman I was.

I sighed again.

"What are you so gloomy about?" Mama cut in, picking up my pile of peeled sweets and examining them as if I would get sloppy and leave the skin on in spots, "We need five more, Lenora, and do tell me what you are sighing about."

My throat tightened, and so did my hands, fingers pressing harder into the knife. I didn't dare confess to Mama the truth, but I didn't have anything to say in its place. No lies were forthcoming. After racing through disjointed thoughts that wouldn't make a coherent reason, I settled on something.

"I just wish we could go to the Arena, Mama." As I suspected, I heard a clicking sound from Mama's tongue. She was about to tell me all the reasons we women didn't go to the Arena even though our family owned it. I cut her off before she could delve into how proper young women didn't go to establishments like that. "I only want to see it, and it can't be all that bad. You used to fight when you were younger. Jonathan told me that's how you met Papa."

Now she laughed, a little low and thick. I glanced over to see that she never stopped mashing the sweets for bread.

"That was a long time ago, Lenora, and I only did it because I was orphaned and starving on the streets. It felt like a better option than whoring myself." She stayed concentrated on the mashing, occasionally she'd add a bit of flour to the mix and then mash some more. "You are not in the position I was in, Lenora. You have a proper family and safety. You'll never have to worry about finding food or money. So there is no need for you to go to the Arena."

I finished peeling the last of the sweets in silence and then joined Mama in kneading the dough, but I couldn't help and sigh again. With her mismatched eyes and keen look, my Mama glanced in my direction as if giving me a warning about my behavior. It wasn't alright to be wanting something I didn't have because I had everything a young woman could hope for except that I didn't have him.

"Is it alright if I tend the garden today?" I asked quickly. "The mint is ready to be harvested, and so are the sugar pods."

"After we get the bread in the oven," Mama replied by putting one doughy lump in a baking pan. I listened to Mama, and as soon as I could, ran out into our little garden. All raised planters facing the sea. It was peaceful here. I had nothing but my basket of mint and sugar pods and the sound of the ocean behind me.

I was clipping the tops of our onions when Lukas strode up to me.

"Hey," He rumbled, a beautiful voice strumming through my soul. I glanced over to him, enthralled by his half there smile.

"Hey," I whispered back a little lower than I intended. "What are you doing back home so early?"

"I came to get lunches. Mama said the bread wasn't done baking yet, though." He shrugged his shoulders and took another step closer to me. Hands reaching out, he lifted my chin softly. "So, I thought I'd come to see how you were doing while I waited."

My tongue tangled, my hands shook. Lukas was getting closer and closer, and I was falling down this hole of heat and lust. Then he stopped while our faces were just a breath apart.

I stopped and stilled and left my heart pounding so loud I was sure it could be heard throughout the whole city.

"Kiss me?" I stammered breathlessly, and he did. His lips molded over mine, sweet and deep pressure. There was a whoosh in my chest as everything turned topsy turvy. Very slowly, the pressure came off, Lukas pulled away from me, and I stared into his beautiful blue eyes, thinking that this man was the only man I would ever love, our current predicament as brother and sister be damned.

"Tomorrow Mama is going to the market," Lukas whispered, and I almost didn't catch it because his hands were slipping down, over my jawline to the top of my chest, until after the barest moment of hesitation, he cupped my breasts through the pink organza and cotton gown I wore. I stood there shocked for a second at the touch, which felt altogether scandalous and sexy at the same time.

"Y-yes," I stuttered, a renewal of heat pilling up in my belly. "Mama wanted to get pickled star jellies for Papa's birthday celebration." His hands didn't let go, squeezing softly, back and forth. He found my nipples through the thin summer gown and twirled them with his thumbs.

"I'm going to come home while she's out." Kisses lined my jaw, and I gasped at his words. Us, alone? I wasn't a child, I knew what would happen if we were alone. I was sure if

Lukas didn't think it was such a risk, he'd have me in the garden right now, and I'd invite it.

I think I would have said something back to him as soon as my head stopped swimming, but that was all so far away when he pulled away from me abruptly, and a moment later, Mama came around the corner.

"Are you done gardening, Lenora?" She asked, but in my mind, it felt like she was asking if I was done being groped by my brother. I was sure my embarrassment was evident on my face. All I could feel was a fire in my cheeks.

"I have a little more to do. I was just talking with Lukas about the Arena."

"Oh, you and your obsession with the Arena. It is not that wonderful of a place. Lukas, tell her about how the toilets haven't been updated to a flush system yet, and every few hours, you need to pull a manual crank to turn on the water and clear them."

Lukas laughed and reached up to scratch his head.

"It isn't all that glamorous, Lenora. Mama's right." I pretended to pout, just like Mama would expect of me. The truth was I didn't care so much about the Arena. It didn't interest me beyond knowing that it belonged to our family. Though I thought it would be fun to see what Lukas did for work every day.

"Mama, I think I hear someone knocking on the door." Lukas nodded towards the front of the house. We paused, and sure enough there was the sound of rapid banging reaching our ears.

"Lukas, come with me. I'm not expecting company," Mama sounded cautious as the sound continued.

It turned out the knocking on our door was from the city guard, a brash couple of men wearing orange silk and leather cuirasses with the sun stitched into the front.

"Good day," the man in the front bowed to Lukas. "We've come to inform the residents on this street that King Martin has ordered an evacuation of the area due to a flood threat."

I peeked out the windows to the blue sky, puzzled. There wasn't even a drop of rain, a single cloud in sight. Mama laughed,

"A flood threat? Young man, even in the heaviest summer rains, this side of the peninsula doesn't flood. It all goes to the south side. I think you are lost."

"Sorry, Ma'am, we are just relaying the information we were told. Evacuations must be complete by nightfall. Good luck to you." The guard bowed properly and then left with his entourage to the next house down the street.

I looked at Mama, Lukas looked at Mama. Both of us were unsure what steps to take.

"Dead Gods," Mama swore, her hands on her hips and a scowl on her face. "King Martin is a mad man. I don't care what he says. We aren't evacuating."

"But the guards?" Lukas questioned, "There're plenty of rooms under the Arena until King Martin lifts the evacuation order. I'd rather not be forcibly removed from our home."

I looked back to Mama whose shoulders slacked in the moment.

"Ohhhhh, alright." She capitulated, "Lukas you need to help Lenora, and I get things together. We are taking valuables with us."

I swallowed my nerves and helped my family prepare for a flood that was never going to come.

Chapter Three

I USUALLY ONLY SAW the Arena once a year, at the Day of Fools celebration when I was allowed to go with Mama to watch all the dancers sail over the stone floor. I had fond memories of the festival, all the way from when I was a child to the last summer when I first noticed Lukas liked me.

My cheeks flushed, and I kept sweeping the grand floor. I couldn't help imagining my startled reaction when we found out about our mutual attraction. I had slipped on the steps going down from the stadium, right into Lukas's arms. We looked at each other, standing there at the base, me with a twisted ankle, and him grasping my bottom to hold me up. The shock and sense of butterflies in my stomach had nearly overpowered me. If only I had known in those moments what I was about to do in these.

"Lenora!"

I swung around to see Lukas motioning to me from the Arena's grand arches. The doorway that led to the city was open, and the sun was shining bright on everything but him. Looking around, I could see no one else in the early morning sunshine. Good, I thought and quickly abandoned my broom to jog over to him.

"Good morning, Lukas!" I chirped, smiling up at him. He had a mischievous grin on his face, his blond hair uncombed and wild on his head.

"Hey, Mama's sending me back to the house to grab an extra set of clothing for everyone. Apparently, the city guards are saying we are going to be here for a while. You want to come with me?"

My pulse sped up, and I leaned forward, "Does Mama know I'm going with you?"

"No," He whispered, "Our secret, Lenora. Do you want to come or not?"

I shivered because it felt like he meant those words in more than one way. It felt like a promise of passion, and I jumped for it.

"Yes, I'll go with you."

His beautiful smile drove me right out the doors of the Arena. We walked along the street down to our home together, and I couldn't help but giggle in unrestrained glee. Lukas reached out and grabbed my hand.

"What are you giggling about?" he teased. I could see the city guard had set up a blockade on the road blocking the two streets closest to the ocean off in the distance. It sobered me a little, but I smiled up to Lukas's perfect face anyway.

"Us, sneaking off like this. It makes me have butterflies in my stomach." I confessed.

"And why would it do that?" He prodded and poked, demanding more of an answer from me. Demanding I clarify when clarifying would be sure to bring a blush to my cheeks.

"Lukas," I breathed out his name, feeling the heat rise in me, "I'm shy." My squeaked words just made him laugh, but he didn't poke anymore because we came upon the guards.

"Halt!" One said, authority strong in his voice. "This area is off-limits."

"Hello," Lukas said with a short bow, "My family resides on Sea Avenue 1.Our parents have asked us to come here and retrieve some clothes for the family as the evacuation orders have been extended."

Two of the guards looked at each other and shrugged.

"You may pass. Don't stay in the evacuation zone too long. King Martin is sure the flood is coming soon."

I glanced at the pale blue sky, the only clouds were over the distant Visoto Mountains, and I wondered at that. It was so clear I could see the moon's daytime outline and the red glow of the Bloodstar right next to it. I wondered if I had ever seen them so close before?

Lukas tugged me.

"Come on, little sister, looks like we don't have much time." He smiled at the guards while holding me by the elbow, "Thank you, gentlemen, for letting us through. We won't be long. I promise."

And down we ran towards our home on the clearest day of the year.

"I think King Martin is a madman." I mumbled, "If anything, we are going to have a drought because it hasn't rained in more than a week."

Lukas simply shrugged and opened the door to our whitewashed house. The top hinge squeaked the way it always did—comforting sounds to calm my giddy self.

"Come to my room?" He whispered and reached out to grab my hands. "I promise I'll make it worth your while."

I giggled some more, flushed, and couldn't bring myself to say anything witty. I followed Lukas past our open parlor down the hallway that led to all of our bedrooms. His was the first on the right. The smallest room. Mama had it converted from an office to his bedroom when my parents adopted him. I remember how hard she tried to make him feel at home. I remembered how different we were three years ago. We were both awkward teenagers then, but I still found him cute and swallowed down those feelings into my gut because he was my brother. Sisters and brothers don't act like this. They don't lust for each other.

It was forbidden.

It was wrong.

Then why was I celebrating when Lukas shut the door to his room and gathered me up in his arms? Why did everything in me scream that this was right when he pressed his lips to mine? It wasn't our fault my parents adopted him when he was nearly an adult. We shouldn't be punished for that!

I kissed back, my mouth opening. Our tongues touched, and he groaned.

"I want more with you." He whispered. "Can I see you undressed?"

I lost my breath for a moment before boldly stating, "Only if you undress too."

He was able to pull off his clothing much faster than I. I struggled with the buttons at the back of my gown while he yanked off his shirt and pulled down his pants. I fumbled even more because though I had seen him work shirtless before, I had never seen him naked. His cock stuck straight up, tight and ready.

"Ausur's Grace," I swore softly and watched him laugh.

"I'm that beautiful, huh? That you'd evoke the name of a god?"

I almost died when he reached down and stroked his cock a few times. I knew that was what I wanted to do. I wanted to touch it, and feel it, and have him inside me. My sex was so wet I was sure it was seeping through my underwear.

"I think I broke a button," I confessed, my fingers not able to rip any more buttons free, and if that was the case, I wasn't getting out of this dress without being cut out. Good thing the green lace was never my favorite.

Lukas tried with the button for a few seconds and then abandoned it.

"That's alright, here, let me help you." His voice was rough, sexy. His hands lifted my skirt, and I teetered on the edge of embarrassment. He didn't let me stay there for long. He pushed me back towards his bed, flipped up my gown when I fell, and pulled off my underwear, throwing it to the other side of his room where it landed on his writing desk.

For a second, my sensibilities returned, and I tried to close my legs, suddenly embarrassed by the attention, but he held them open, looking down at my lily. His blue eyes drifted back up to my face.

"This isn't just a viewing party, Lenora. I want to take your lily. What do you think?" As he said those words, he pushed his pelvis against my spread legs. It excited me to feel his cock rub on my wet lily. I couldn't help but moan.

"Yes," My voice rumbled out of me. "Please, take me. I've wanted you to for so long."

He kept rubbing against me, his cockhead hitting the bud at the top of my sex. All I felt was a buzzing in my veins, an increase of heat so intense it was almost unbearable. My face was a flush. I was gasping.

"Please, Lukas, put it in me." I tried to spread my petals wider, and it may have worked because he slid in just a bit on his next undulation. Quickly he pulled his hand in and kept rubbing my bud.

"I'm going to ask Papa if I can marry you." He groaned, just a little deeper. I moaned at the slowness, at the pressure. I wanted more, and I wanted his words, but I knew even if he did ask for my hand, he would never get it. It was illegal in Lopuri for siblings to marry, even if they were only related through adoption. What we were doing right now was unlawful, even though it felt so good.

He slid in all the way, filling me slowly. I gasped at the feeling, so right, so sexy. I knew I needed more. My body was humming with excitement. Zing. Zing. Hot. I was almost squirming.

"Lukas," I panted his name, beggingly, "Please, I need more."

He began thrusting, hard, deep. A precise, beautiful pace, racing with my heart. In no time at all, I could feel the heat in me bloom. It was sudden, like lightning. It was spreading up from my lily into my spine, all the way to the top of my head. I tingled. It took my breath away and made my ears flood with the sound of my heartbeat. I was so engulfed that I couldn't be sure I heard correctly in the following moments.

There were booms outside of our home, like the sounds of cannons going off, except the city cannons were never this close to residential areas.

"What was--" I was cut off, Lukas' hand clamped over my mouth and he thrust one more time, groaning as his cock pulsed inside me.

And then I heard it.

The door to his room opened, and in a life-changing moment, Papa and Mama walked in. Where there had been nothing but heat before was ice, fear. I didn't hesitate to scramble up and out from under Lukas. He didn't hesitate to fall backward off his bed and nervously look for his pants.

My hands were tight in the weave of my green dress. I knew they caught us. As if I were some dreadful Rathinian girl, my parents witnessed my first time. Outside I could still hear cannon shots.

Papa yelled first, and his ire was directed right at me.

"You little whore!"

I shrunk back against the wall as he took two steps toward me. Again outside, I heard an explosion. Papa reached me and, with a balled fist, hit me across the face.

"No! Stop!" Mama yelled, but it did nothing because the next moment I realized water covered my feet.

I looked down with my pained cheek throbbing. Papa looked down. Everyone looked down. The whole floor of Lukas's room was wet and smelled like the ocean.

"What is going on here?" I heard my Mama wonder out loud. I stared down, my cheek stinging with pain, blood pooling in my mouth, and realized in the distance, towards the sea, I could hear the crashing sound of rushing water. The sound of it was coming straight for us.

"Run!" Lukas called out, and we all tried to run through a soup of seawater that was creeping up to our shins out of Lukas's room, through the parlor. The horrifying sound of a water wall was getting worse, engulfing everything else, including the pace of my terrified heart. I made it out of the front door with my Mama's help. She yanked up my wet gown and placed the heavy material in my hands so I could run. Sort of run, splash through the sea that rose past its boundaries. I panicked in my inadequacy to get out.

"Lenora!" Lukas yelled my name, and I looked up to see him and Papa were running to the tree in our front yard. Lukas began to climb it when I noticed the sky was tinted red. Streaks of fire were falling all around us. A neighbor's palm thatch roof ignited, which felt strange because everything else was wet. My mind tumbled, realizing it had started raining when it was so sunny not that long ago.

"Lenora! Come here!" Lukas screamed at me, and I tried. I was too shocked to feel much of anything. I ran to the tree too, hugged the trunk, and looked back just in time to see a massive wall of water, tinted red by the streaks of fire in the sky.

Lukas was grabbing my arms, trying to pull me up into the tree. When the wave crashed into the back of the house, sickening crunches filled the air, and the water was too fast. In seconds the water was up to my neck. And seconds later, it was trying to return to the sea, trying its best to drag me along with it. Mama was knocked back towards the broken whitewash, I was pulled hard by the rushing wave, my fingers getting cut by the wet tree bark, and the only reason I wasn't sucked back was because of Lukas's hands held tight over my arms.

Sickeningly I looked out and screamed, "Mama!"

I could see her floating in the water, being pulled back with the broken debris of our home, blood dripping down over her face. I could see and numbly knew there was nothing in the world I could do to save her as the sea retreated and

brought with it everything I had ever known.

Chapter Four

WE HELD ON TIGHT for wave after pounding wave. I almost let go. I almost had to when pieces of broken house snagged my dress underwater seeking to drag me along with it. But somehow, I managed to hold on, fingers aching. I was simultaneously terrified and numb, watching helplessly as the sky shot flames from the moon that exploded over our heads.

It was hours of silence between Papa, Lukas, and me. Just us watching the end of the world, not the romantic scenery I had always imagined would happen after my first time. It was hours of looking out frantically over the waters, hoping beyond hope that we would see Mama come in with one of the smaller waves. That we might have the grace of gods on our side and be able to save her.

Instead, as my arms shook with the effort to hold onto the tree any longer, the guard rescued us.

"Citizens!" One of the guard's men called out. "We'll help you!"

And before I knew it, the guard tossed a rope in our direction, rough, wet through the slop of the sea that hadn't completely retreated. It hurt to loosen my grip from the tree, and Lukas hissed at me.

"Can't you move any faster?" I cringed at his words because I couldn't move faster. My arms and legs were petrified from having born the brunt of sea surf for hours while he and my father simply sat in the tree. Lukas let go of me long ago. *Why didn't they pull me up to save me?* I wondered and then achy but dutifully helped them to the rope.

One at a time, they climbed down the tree, and with all three of us holding onto the rope, the guards guided us up to the higher street level, almost in our neighbor's yard.

"There are shelters at the grand cathedral and the church of the sea." One guard spoke lightly when we were out of the water. My Papa shook his head and mutely waved a hand to the speaking man. His wet boots were already tromping down the road towards the Arena.

"Dead Gods, I hope the Arena is alright." I wrung out my skirts to get rid of the heavy water and prepared to run after Papa.

"If it isn't, it's your fault." Lukas sneered, and his words got Papa to turn around even though he was already a few paces away from us. It made the guards quiet and observant. "If you hadn't seduced me, none of this would have happened."

"W-what do you mean?" I questioned, hurt. It speared through my delicate heart. For the first time, I saw Lukas sneer. It wasn't a pretty look on his face. It made all the manly parts of him look dangerous.

"You made me have sex with you even though it's against God to have sex with a sibling. If it weren't for you, the ocean wouldn't have swallowed our house. Mama wouldn't be dead! You are nothing but a little sex-driven whore."

"Lukas, that's enough," Papa called out. "We are going home."

I watched. My face was hot with embarrassment as Lukas looked down on me once more and then turned to catch up with Papa. I was numb, stuck in place, watching the sea come in and out, red waves, as red as blood. This couldn't be my fault, could it?

One of the guards was whispering about me. I heard the word "girl" and caught him pointing at how my dress stuck to me in indecent ways. There was a sudden flash of danger there, and I ran to catch up to Papa even though I wasn't sure that was much safer.

He did hit me, after all.

The three of us walked in silence until we got to the Arena. My little brother, Mateo, was sitting out on the front step anxiously waiting for us. Tears pouring down his young face. He looked like he had seen the world end even though it was clear no water reached this place.

"Papa!" he screamed and then bolted to our father, wrapping his skinny arms around him. Papa stopped and patted his head for a second before gruffly speaking.

"Go get Jonathan."

Mateo complied, running back into the Arena where Papa blocked off the entrance with his big strong body. My mouth ran dry. Why not just let everyone in? Why not let us go to bed? There was housing in the lower floors reserved for Arena fighters during the season, and our season wasn't supposed to start for another two weeks.

Eventually, though, Jonathan and Mateo emerged, both looking worried. Papa gave them no time. He dove in with all the expectation of quick recovery, like the fighter he had once been.

"Your mother is dead." He announced, and even though I knew it to be true, it crushed my heart into jagged pieces, and I cried again. Fat tears floating down my face, I almost didn't hear the rest of his words. "Lukas, you are no longer welcome in this family."

"But my inheritance."

"You forfeited it when you snuck off with my daughter!" Papa bellowed, "Now get out of here before I call the guards on you for trespassing!"

My shoulders were stiff. I didn't know what to think. Giving Lukas nothing but the clothes on his back seemed such a horrible fate, but I was still broken up over his earlier words: my *fault, my fault, my fault.* I ruined a man's life by wanting him, by having him. And he believed that I changed the world into the hell around us.

"Lenora," Papa said my name sharply, "Your sins are why we are here now. Are you happy, girl?"

Mutely, I shook my head in the negative. No, despite my daydreams having sex with Lukas had not made me happy at all. Doing what we did put us in danger, put Mama and Papa in trouble, and now Mama was dead! The one person I may have been able to talk to about my feelings was gone.

I cried some more.

"Stop that," Papa commanded to no avail. The tears were here, and they were staying, "Lenora and Mateo, we are going to move up north. My brother has a farm just north of South Cross. We are going to go live there. Jonathan, you have the Arena."

"Yes, Papa," Jonathan said dutifully, but I could feel my older brother bore holes through me with his eyes. It made me stuck and scared until Papa demanded I go inside and go to sleep in the same room as Mateo, but on the way by my big brother, I heard him say it, "Whore." His voice with such deep vehemence that I didn't know the label would ever leave me.

Chapter Five

SOME DAYS I KNEW when things weren't going my way. Once my favorite dress tore, and I knew the day was spoiled. Once my little brother put slugs on my morning toast, and I predicted a day of stomach problems. Earlier, less than a week ago, I made love to a man and was caught by my parents. I didn't know what prediction to make there, didn't realize that my life was going to be turned upside down in more ways than I could imagine. Shortly thereafter, the sea rose and swallowed our house. Every time I close my eyes, I can still see the deafening grumbling churn of water rushing into the street. I didn't know I'd see the waves carry my mother away never to be with us again.

Those were big things. Things that scared my delicate heart. And I didn't know there was going to be a snowball smashing into the back of my head as a result of it all. It made me scream shrilly, my voice bouncing off of the sheer mountain peaks around us.

"Lenora! Don't shriek. You'll cause an avalanche, just like you cause everything bad to happen." My father sounded exhausted when he spoke. Dead tired, bone-weary, and mean. I couldn't blame him. My chest felt hollow, my fingers ached, and I bowed my head when I spoke.

"Sorry, Papa, Mateo hit me..."

"He is just a child. Let him play." Father's words were firm, holding no recourse for me. No reprimand for my little brother. Yes, Mateo was a child, but I wasn't so much older than him. I had only turned 19 a week before the sea rose and swallowed our home. Before the skies rained fire and Mother died causing our family to split apart. Back to that again, I wondered if remembering it would ever go away.

Maybe, I thought. Once I was away from Lopuri forever. Papa decided that we were moving after two days with no home. He left the Arena to Jonathan and cut Lukas out of the family altogether. The last I saw of my former lover, he was hanging around the Arena entrance, probably contemplating what life as a beggar would be like. And Lukas deserved it.

"Don't be so sour, Lenora. You used to have fun with me, and now you're just boring." Mateo wiggled his hands in my hair, spreading more slushy snow in my brown braid. I didn't appreciate my brother's joking but didn't say anything. With any luck, he wouldn't hit me with a snowball again. With any luck, our short passage through the mountains was almost at an end.

"Lenora, look up ahead. There are the lights of Elevar."

I lifted my head to see the famed castle in the mountains. It was huge, made of grey mountain stone and shimmering marble; black towers rose to the sky where it looked like they'd get engulfed by the clouds themselves. Lanterns hung on the outside walls, in well-spaced intervals, making the whole long shape of the castle glow golden.

Right in front of us was a drawbridge, though I didn't understand why they had one, except maybe aesthetics. There was nothing to climb over to get to the door. But the bridge was down and inviting. I shivered in the near nightfall of the mountain pass but doubted that my Father would have us stop here.

As pretty as Elevar was, it was not a place for upstanding men, not a place for children, and not a place for a proper young woman. It was a place of salacious rumors and things I could barely think of without blushing. Maybe that's why I began to predict trouble as my father trudged through the snow, up onto the shoveled drawbridge, to the front door.

"Papa?" I called out worriedly.

"It's just an inn, Lenora. We won't make it to the other side of the mountain pass tonight, and there aren't any other safe havens up here." His shoulder's looked stiff, and I could tell he was telling himself this as much as he was telling me. It made my stomach swirl with unsettled feelings.

"It's just a castle," Mateo huffed and ran up to our Father. I doubted he had ever heard anything about Elevar. He was only twelve, far too young to be listening to rumors about whores.

Seeing as there was no other option besides staying out in the cold, I followed my father and brother. Every footstep made an enormous pit sit in my stomach. I didn't like this idea, shelter from the snow or not. We were all healthy, all able-bodied. We could push through the mountains into the flatlands below and sleep there in the morning. Or we could just go home and make a new home. Why, oh why, did we have to leave? My cheeks flushed, and I knew the answer. We left because Papa blamed Lukas and me for Mama's death. He couldn't stand staying there without her, and if he kept me quiet about my sexual indiscretions, he might still be able to sell me off to a proper young man because of our name.

"Oh, dears, come in from the cold!" the voice from

inside wasn't at all what I was expecting. She was soft and sweet, not devilishly sultry or trying to get our Father's coin. "Anni! Hurry up and grab some blankets! There are children here!"

I supposed they thought I was younger. I was short, only a scant bit taller than my little brother, and since the silk shawl I managed to snag from Mama's clothes was so big, I was sure it hid the other signs of my maturity. My breasts, after all, were not childlike.

We were ushered inside the ample open space of the entrance. It was as opulent inside as out, with redwood walls, vast paintings of fruit and flowers all over the walls. I had never been inside a castle before but couldn't believe how cozy the wealth seemed. There were couches and shayes and seats all around, not many people, though. Just a few women who jumped into action as if our arrival indicated a change in their routine.

I stepped in closer to my father, hardly listening as he spoke with the woman who let us in. She was an older sort, with silver hair done up in a big bun on the top of her head. She didn't look like a whore, or at least not what I imagined a whore to look like. She was just a woman, and I noticed she was wearing a heavy blue coat over her dress and was carrying two pails of snow at her side. I wondered what the snow was for.

"Yes, we saw the sky light on fire up here too," I listened to her silky voice croon, "My, that is terrifying that the sea rose past the surge walls. How much of the city is left?"

"Most of it," My father replied, "All the northern half, anyway."

"Just not your home." The words were horrifyingly spoken as if she was personally sad for our loss. Maybe she was, but no amount of stunned strangers could take away the memories. For a second, I stood there and shook, remembering how my mother's face had blood on it when bobbed out with the rest of the waves. I wondered if she died drowning or bleeding.

Before me, my father shook his head silently, but I didn't think he would cry. He didn't cry ever, not even when he realized not all of us made it.

"We're heading north to go live with Uncle Sam and Auntie Janna!" My brother butted in. The woman looked over to him and then glanced at me. My fingers felt like ice around the silk shawl, red like the ocean coming in to kill us. I shook off the urge to drop it. My clothing underneath was sleeveless because home was always hot. I had only ever owned a sleeved gown once when we went north to visit family.

"Traveling through these mountains with children, a sign of bad times, good sir. Here, let me bring you to your room."

I wondered for a second why payment hadn't been discussed but decided to keep my mouth shut. That was between my father and her, not my business. Or so I thought.

We were shuffled up a flight of stairs and off to the right side hallway. Down we went all the way almost to the end. The room the woman gave us wasn't much. It had one big bed and a couch inside and a fireplace that Father immediately went towards lighting.

"Toilets are just a little further down the hall on the left for you men," The woman spoke and then turned to me, "I'm sorry, my dear, but you will have to use the bathrooms downstairs by the front doors. There are no girls allowed in the men's toileting area."

I nodded quietly but still didn't speak.

"Lenora, speak your gratitude," my father demanded. I bowed and wondered why I was being singled out. Why not my brother? Shouldn't we all be saying thanks and praise for being let in from the snow?

We could have kept walking.

"Thank you for your hospitality." I kept myself in line. It wasn't hard to. I felt a little numb and a little rushed through all this. I didn't hear whatever words came from the woman's mouth, focused only on the call of a warm bed.

"Don't take all the blankets!" Mateo complained as I shimmied into a spot. I curled into myself, kicking off the top layer of blankets so that my brother wouldn't cry. I listened to what was left of my family settle down around me. My father on the couch, Mateo sprawled out on the bed, and I... I just looked at the cloth wallpaper, past the pastel flowers on the wall, imagining watching the sea come in to take me.

Chapter Six

SLEEP WAS BLESSEDLY SILENT for me. Calm, and not full of screams or chaos, or people shaking me awake. Shaking me awake...

I opened my eyes to see the same woman who helped us in from last night standing over me, except now she wasn't wearing a heavy coat. Her gown was a daring orange like the setting sun, drop shoulders and low on the bustline showing off the curve of her breasts. Something more like what I thought a whore would wear.

"Good morning, Lenora, I let you sleep in after all you've been through, but you really must wake up now." She almost sang the words as if she was a songbird outside my window and not a stranger standing over me as I struggled to open my eyes after sleep.

I reached out to Mateo. Mateo wasn't there.

"Papa?" I called, "Mateo?" But there was no answer, and that pit that I felt when first coming upon Elevar sunk in deeper into my stomach. The woman above me made a soft sound, soothing almost.

"My darling, your Papa didn't tell you, did he?"

I couldn't breathe. I was still looking for some sign of them in the room. Their shoes by the door, Mateo's hat on the coat hook. Nothing. Nothing. It was as if the sea had taken them too, reached up into the mountains, and dragged them into the blue to die with Mother.

My panic swirled up with such dizzying wonderment that I was hardly aware of it when the woman reached out and grabbed my hands. Her fingers were calloused like Mother's, and feeling her rub them over my shaking fingers calmed me down. It pulled me back and made me know I wasn't by the sea. I was up in a castle, left behind by my very father.

"Why did my Papa leave me behind?" My first question to her was stilted with crying. I sounded like a gasping ghastly mess, but the woman just shushed me more, rubbing my hands in that motherly way.

"I imagine there were a few reasons, my dear," She hushed me, "He inquired about how much an apprenticeship in Elevar would bring in for money. I don't think that decision was light on his mind."

"He sold me?" I choked. So he believed Lukas's hateful accusations after all.

"Oh, you are a free woman; if you choose to go, you may. But it was your father's wish that you work for us and send a portion of your pay to him while your family is trying to re-establish their home."

I sat there stunned, heartbroken. I was left behind in the most famous whore house in the world to make money for my family. Despite what this woman said, I knew the truth. Papa wasn't going to sell me off to a nice young man. He believed I was a whore when I simply thought I fell in love. If I sent even one coin to my family, I would never be welcome back. I was already not marriage material. Papa cast me out. And if I ran after him without a coin to show, who knew what might happen?

My throat hurt, and I remembered the moment he walked in and caught Lukas and me having sex. I remembered the strike of his fist and wondered if my only options were what he decided? Be a whore, or die? I just stared at the woman wondering how she could have let a father walk off without his child? How could she have let me become payment?

She smiled at me.

"My name is Ava. Come, eat some food. I doubt you've had a good meal lately."

I hadn't, but I didn't trust her. I felt sore in my heart, a deep betrayal bleeding through all the pieces of me.

"I don't want to be a whore." I blurted out as Ava got up off the bed.

"Well, there are plenty of jobs that will get you money in Elevar, little Lenora," Ava said softly, "You might get lonely flushing the toilets all day, though."

I didn't know what she meant by that then, but a few hours later, after eating a meager breakfast of flour cakes and sweet wine, I was sent outside with buckets and showed how to clear the toilets in Elevar.

They had a broken pump system. I don't know why they didn't repair it, but the only way to flush the long line of toilets was to boil snow on the stove, slowly, until it turned to water and then dump heavy bucket after heavy bucket down the system, all day long.

Halfway through the day, my arms ached from lifting buckets of water and snow, and the shock of numbness that permeated me upon waking and finding I was left behind had started to dissipate, replaced by a horrified acceptance that this was the way things were going to be. I went outside one more time, shoveling up snow into the buckets with my hands. Thankfully Ava had let me borrow a pair of mittens. I looked around me and saw the mountain pass. It was easy to see up here, narrow down to the city of Lopuri, my home by birth, where it was always hot and never saw snow. There was another narrow path twisting north, the footprints of my father and brother still clear outlines in the snow. I blinked back tears looking at them. And then there was a third wider path that led east towards the wild countryside. I knew I didn't want to go there, but as I packed down the snow in my bucket, I couldn't help but look at the path back home.

Jonathan and Lukas were still there. I bit my lip and worried. Jonathan probably wouldn't take me in. I know how he felt about what happened. My oldest brother personally assisted in chasing Lukas away from the Arena when he tried to come back and plead his case and hadn't said a single word to me before Papa dragged me up to the mountains.

I couldn't go back to Lukas, we'd both be begging in the streets, and I knew he'd never be able to look at me after everything that happened. If I was honest, I don't know that I'd be able to see him the same after he turned on me.

"Lenora!" Ava called to me from the doorway. "Come inside. It's going to get too cold to be out here soon. Look, there's a storm coming in through the mountain pass."

I glanced to where she was pointing and saw the dark clouds sailing serenely through the sky. Grabbing up the buckets of snow, I struggled to carry them back in and refused to take a last look at Papa and Mateo's footprints.

Thankfully Ava grabbed up one bucket and helped me bring it into the kitchen. My numb fingers let go of my bucket with a plop, and tiredly, I went to turn on the coal stove.

"You know if you join us, days like this would be fewer. There are 5 of us residing here, and normally we split the chores." Ava spoke as if those words would make me feel better, but it was too soon, and my life terribly upended.

"I'm not ready for this," I whispered, but she heard me anyway.

"Your father seemed to think you'd get along well here. What happened to make him think that about you?" The question made my stomach feel weird. I couldn't help the blush that dredged up on my cheeks and the memory of passion and pleasure. My tongue was tied. I had no desire to relive those moments because it was already difficult enough to admit that they led me here.

If only I hadn't gone with Lukas. He might have grabbed the clothes for our family and came back to the Arena before the sea took our home. Maybe none of that would have happened at all if I didn't have sex with my brother.

Maybe Mama would still be alive.

"It's all my fault." I choked on my tears.

"What is your fault?" Ava asked, her calm voice in my periphery. Shaking my head, I tried to go back to work, but the damage was already done, and she invested herself in my business. "What do you think is your fault, girl? Were you taken against your will? Is that why your father dropped you off here as if you were ruined?"

I heaved a sob and turned to her with upset.

"It's my fault the sky rained with fire, and the sea swallowed up the land. It's my fault Mama is dead! None of that would have happened if I hadn't snuck off to have sex with my adopted brother!"

For a moment, there was quiet, and I questioned myself. There were limits that whores didn't even cross. I wondered if I made a mistake when Ava grabbed me by my arm. She held me with hard hands and scowled at me.

I worried that I just bought my way out into the snow. I'd never survive on my own, but she surprised me.

"Those things are not your fault." Her voice had taken on a new quality, no longer calm, a little frayed around the edges. "Dear Lenora, I'm sorry fate has brought you here. Do you want to know how I came to be here?"

I didn't care, but I nodded out of politeness.

"My father sold me here, back when girls were handpicked and purchased by the owner." I watched her take a deep breath, her dark eyes swimming with unnamed emotions. "My own father signed up to be my first client, and I was helpless. The world doesn't turn upside down when you have sex with family."

"But it did for me." I retorted. "Fire..."

"Yes, yes, I'm aware of what happened. We saw the Bloodstar crash into the moon up here too." Ava waved me off, "It still has nothing to do with whatever you were doing at that moment. It's just bad luck. And you, Lenora, are not in the same position I was in. As soon as I earned enough money and I became old enough, I took over this fine establishment. I don't buy girls' bodies and force them to work for my money back. Everyone here is here because they've chosen to be. So, Lenora, you can work for us if you want, and if you don't, I can have a friend bring you back to Lopuri."

The snow had almost completely melted on the stovetop and now was beginning to boil as I struggled to find words, nay thoughts. What this woman offered me was against everything I had ever been taught, but it provided safety that at the current moment I did not have. I bit my lip and thought about Mama. What would she say if she was alive?

I didn't know, but I suspected that she wouldn't have cast me out of the family for my misdeeds. All my life I learned how she felt about the things that she did to survive before marrying my father. I knew she found strength in fighting in the Arena, but that option was unlikely to happen for me. Mama was strong and brash, and I... I was her daughter, as strong as she was. There was no way I could have done what she did because Jonathan would block it, but I would make it through this. I decided that she wouldn't judge me for not being able to do those things.

Hesitantly, I pulled the first bucket of water off the stove and struggled to put the second one up to warm it. Ava was still watching me, quietly, as if waiting for my answer.

"How..." I stumbled, searching for words, "How does this work? If I agree to be employed as a --."

"Lady in the mountain." Ava cut me off from vulgar words. Lady in the mountain, she made it sound dignified to spread my legs for men willing to pay me. "Darling, there are many reasons why men come to Elevar. It's not all sex and debauchery. Many travelers use our rooms as an inn, and there are many hats you can try on here. The ten of us do all the upkeep for the castle, cooking, cleaning, and entertaining. We have two dancers, a singer, and a magician. Most of the time, our tasks are those sort of things rather than private entertainment, but we would train you in that as well. Those who do come to us for pleasure expect expertise and not virginity."

I watched the snow slowly melting and came to a conclusion that hurt.

"This is the only option left to me in life." I looked back to Ava. The older woman had taken a chair to sit in for our conversation. She smiled at my words and leaned forward.

"Lenora, soon you will find that it is not a bad cast in life. I promise you."

Chapter Seven

IT WAS A WEEK before my training began. Ava said it was because not many people traveled the passes this time of year, and the other women in the castle agreed.

"Good thing you came to us during the slow season," Elevar's renowned singer Marie said to me with a mischievous grin. The young woman was only a few years older than me and loved wearing gowns with big feathers stuck into the beadwork. She looked like a peacock and acted like one too.

"Marie, don't try to scare her." Elevar's twin dancers, Clara and Bella, spoke simultaneously, a creepy practice that they sought because laying with two beautiful women at once was a turn-on for some men. I ignored all the teasing preferring instead to dust the bookshelf of the main parlor. I glanced at the titles and was excited to see a vast variety of literature, both old and new available right at my fingertips. I'd have to ask Ava if it was alright if I borrowed a book or two before bed.

"Lenora, are you ready?" The girl who called me was beautiful. She had the prettiest black hair I had ever seen, shiny and straight. Her face was round and sweet, perpetually childlike, and she was a Rathinian... well, half-Rathinian from what Ava told me. Anni Kathe was born in Elevar in the same year I was born. Her mother had been the only Rathinian whore in the house before her, and Ava said that she died in childbirth with the father fleeing north instead of facing his duties as the father to a new baby girl. Faced with no other option, Ava raised Anni to be a discerning businesswoman and the most sought-after girl in all of Elevar.

Now, it was my turn to learn from her. I smiled and put down the dusting rag on an end table. My heart was racing in nervous anticipation.

"I am ready." My voice wobbled inside my throat, and I was sure I didn't sound ready at all, but Anni simply nodded at me. Where her adopted mother was warm and open, she was a bit more distant. I heard the other girls say that though Anni had rarely seen any other Rathinians, she trained to take on their mannerisms. Cold, aloof, and fiercely passionate behind closed doors.

I was a little frightened. I couldn't help it as I followed Anni to her room.

"My client is one of our regulars," Anni spoke softly. I had to strain just to hear her voice as we came upon her room. "Now, there are always proper steps to take before entertaining men. You should always bathe before your appointment time. Strong perfumes are not ideal for a woman's body. Always tidy up your room, and make sure your entertaining sheets are on."

"Entertaining sheets?" I asked, baffled. Anni opened her door and invited me inside. Her room was twice the size of the one I had been given. Her bed had tall posters draped in expensive yellow silk, and there was a trunk at the bottom of her bed covered with shining leather.

"Yes, of course, you don't have any yet." Anni nodded sagely, "I suppose Ava won't expend the money on entertaining sheets until you have completed training, but you should know anyway. You'll have your normal bedding for when the nights are just your own and two sets of entertaining sheets for when you have company. Those sheets are stain-resistant because most of the time, men are messy."

My cheeks heated up, and I suddenly understood what she was saying.

"Of course..." I replied.

"Now come help me prepare." I did my tasks, helping her along as she changed her bedding and tidied up her room. Not that there was much tidying to be done, it looked like she was a sensibly clean person all of the time.

I was almost done sweeping her floor when she called me to her side again. This time she stood next to the leather trunk in her room, hands crossed gently in front of her.

"Usually when you have a regular come and visit, you will already know what sorts of things they enjoy. Until you learn them, you can ask any one of us for guidance and sometimes supplies."

I watched as she lifted open the lid to her trunk. Inside were various ropes, boards, and an amalgamation of materials that looked suspiciously like a man's cock. Stone and wood. All stiff and ready forever. Rich statues to blush at. Anni yanked out ropes that were dyed a bright purple and closed the rest of the chest.

"What do you need ropes for?" I questioned. My mind was flat as the sea on a calm day trying to figure it out. Anni hummed and held the purple ropes lovingly.

"Today, I need them for you. Our client for this afternoon gets skittish if there are other people in the room. So when training needs to happen, the trainee gets tied up to ease his mind. Now get undressed so that I can put you in a bind."

I hesitated, heart palpitating, my throat stuck, "I thought I was here to watch."

"You are." She smiled prettily and showed off the ropes, "But watching invites participation. Trust me; this is for the best."

I didn't entirely trust her. My nerves were on edge, but I let her tie me up anyway. I let her undress me for the task. Every brush of the ropes against my skin zinged into me. Strangely it excited me in a weird anticipatory way. I couldn't help but wonder if Lukas ever would have wanted me like this? But then I chased those thoughts away because Lukas, while he had lusted after me, had no experience with women. He never had any reason to know the tricks of whores, and it was only by circumstance that now I needed to know these things.

"Don't tense up," Anni said, securing the last rope. I was kneeling on the plush carpet of her room, knees pulled apart, thighs wrangled to my calves, and my hands pulled behind me.

"I'm trying not to," I looked up at her with a blush staining my cheeks. "I'm nervous."

She giggled and patted the top of my head with her hand.

"Oh, why? Because you are naked? Lenora, I'm going to be doing all the work. You just get to watch and show off those beautiful breasts of yours." She walked around the side of her big bed as she spoke, pulling off the silk robe she wore to lounge in. Nervously I looked and refused to turn my head away even though she wore no underwear underneath. Her breasts were smaller than mine and tipped up to the sky with their perk.

This is my own doing, remember? I watched silently as Anna got ready. She spread oils on her skin, making it luminous in the candlelight. She played with her breasts, and to my curious embarrassment, laid down on her bed to play with her lily as we waited for her client to get here.

My face was flushed, and the familiar feeling of arousal pulled straight through my pelvis as I watched her. It confused me; shouldn't I only feel that way for Lukas? Or at the least someone I loved? But I felt it rushing through my veins, making my head dizzy as she swirled her fingers around and around her spread petals.

She must have noticed my staring because in a breathy, aroused voice she laughed at me, "It is a good idea to help yourself before a client comes in. They aren't always here for your pleasure, only their own."

I didn't know what to make of those words because I had naively thought that sex was always pleasurable for both parties. Maybe that was just what I wanted. It seemed I was going to learn a lot today. The door to Anni's room opened, and in walked the darkest man I had ever seen in my life. His skin was like an eclipse, though his clothes indicated he lived north. A wool shirt with a birch button front and leather pants that had worn out around his knees. He tied his black hair back in many different braids, the ends tipped with multi-colored glass beads.

When he looked toward the bed, I was shocked to see marks on his face like fractals of lightning over his cheekbones. They glowed orange for a second and then faded away to almost blend in with his skin.

A demon.

I had seen demons before, of course. The Rathinian Empire was full of them. Every summer season, the wealthy elite of the Rathinian Empire voyaged to my home in Lopuri for a vacation away from their summer monsoons. But despite seeing demons around the city, I had never once interacted with one.

"Kameron," Anni spoke softly, "You're late this year."

The demon laughed softly.

"Were you counting down the days till my arrival, Anni?"

"Always," Anni said, but I felt it was probably a lie. I doubted very much that she cared for this client any more than any other. Anni was a professional whore, after all. There was no reason she wouldn't say whatever she thought a man would want to hear. "I even have a little present for you this time."

I felt exposed when the demon slid his dark eyes to me. I could feel them sizing me up, testing my skin, and now I knew the reason behind the ropes. I couldn't run away or hide even if I wanted to. And I very much wanted to when Kameron crouched down beside me. He still towered over me in his hunched-over position. But he didn't reach out and touch me. His hands were still, and he looked into my eyes.

"It's not very often I see new girls in Elevar, and you look so innocent. You remind me of someone." The rumble of his voice broke through my skin and made it stand on edge. I was trying to pay attention to his words, but all I could think was that soon I would see him have sex with Anni. I was going to watch them, and my poor heart might not handle that.

"She's not innocent at all. Ava told me she had sex with her brother, and that's why the Bloodstar died."

Kameron snorted, and I squeaked out, "Adopted brother. We aren't related."

"Regardless of who you've spent intimate moments with the Bloodstar's death isn't your fault." Kameron sounded downright annoyed with his words. "That thing probably crashed on the Moon all by itself. No need to blame girls for their desires over it. That's asinine."

"Oh, Kameron, we didn't mean to make you upset," Anni slid out of her bed and came over to us, hips swaying as she walked. I watched her lacquered fingertips run across Kameron's shoulders. "Come to bed with me."

He turned back to me, and I saw his demon marks light up again, a soft orange white across his face.

"Do you really believe you caused the Bloodstar to crash into the moon?" In the background, Anni mumbled annoyed words in Rathinian. Slowly, I nodded.

"What I did was a sin, and it's why I'm here now. My parents caught us, and then the sea took our house. It took my Mama."

Kameron reached out and smoothed my loose hair back.

"It's not your fault, girl. I'll prove it to you."

Suddenly he was lifting me, carrying me across the room to Anni's bed. I was plopped down right at her pillow, still tied up and unable to move.

"Anni! I haven't seen you love a woman in a long time." Kameron growled. "What about today?"

"Lenora is only supposed to be here for training," Anni replied softly. She still sounded annoyed, as if his attention to me had her jealous. Maybe she had a good reason to be jealous, I thought, for in the next moment, his mouth was on mine seeking a kiss that I hadn't been ready to give.

My heart pumped at a rapid pace; I tried to hold my breath but couldn't. Kameron pulled back slightly, his hand still up in my hair.

"See? The world isn't ending, even though you kissed a demon. I'm sure that wasn't allowed either?"

"I don't know." I squeaked out, embarrassed. He just laughed softly. I liked how gentle his voice was. It made me think I could trust him to kiss me.

"Lenora, Kameron is right. The Bloodstar's death isn't your fault." Anni said, sitting down next to me, "But Kameron, look at how she's shaking. She isn't ready for this yet."

I didn't realize I was shaking, but I noticed it as soon as it was pointed out. My whole body shivered violently, and I thought it was strange because I wasn't cold at all.

"Oh alright," Kameron reached behind me, and a moment later I felt the ties on my wrists come undone, "No need to have you tied up if you aren't ready. You can come or go. It was good to meet you."

I stayed still as the ropes loosened around me. Purple against my skin, though nothing had ever been tight enough to cause bruises. I only inspected my arms and legs for a moment before looking back at Anni and Kameron. They had already started kissing, despite me being there on the bed with them. Kameron's big hand engulfed one of Anna's tiny breasts. I blushed and teetered on the edge of what I should do.

On the one hand, I could put this off, keep doing housework and flushing toilets until I dropped, or I could stay and learn how to become a genuine member of this community. I watched them again. Kameron's hand had slid down between Anni's legs, and I flushed at the sight of his fingers sliding over her lily. Besides, the heat sloshed up between my legs. I was sure my face flushed, but I refused to run.

"I think I'm going to stay," I announced. Kameron looked up from Anni's body and smiled at me.

"Good. I was hoping you would. Now come here and help me make this lily bloom."

I did what he said, complacent, embarrassed but willing. He grabbed my hand and drew it to Anni's lily laughing at me when a new flush came over my cheeks upon touching it. Hand over hand, he guided me into pleasing the woman who was supposed to be training me. Our fingers tangled together as we smoothed down the wet petals. He shoved his inside and lazily pulled them back out, only to repeat the motion. It caught my breath and held it. It was so sexy watching his big dark hands pleasing her, occasionally letting go of his grip to wrap around mine and force me to rub her faster. I found her bud and flicked it back and forth like I occasionally did to myself in the middle of the night when no one was around.

Anni slowly bloomed in sighs and gasps against our hands. She was unrestrained in a way I had never even thought to be. Letting out her desires with a soft moan, I was surprised when she started shaking against me. Trembling.

Sexy and open. I swore I could see the crash of bliss toss her about like a strong wave.

"Oh Anni," Kameron's voice was husky, deeper than it was before. I looked over to him to see that he was pulling off his wool shirt. He was all streamlined muscles, beautiful and sleek. His demon marks cracked down his neck to the defined outline of his chest. I wondered if all demon marks lit up like his. Then he looked at me, and my core shivered. "Your turn, Lenora."

The first time he said my name made me wet. I squeaked when he gently laid me back on the bed and spread my legs. Briefly, I wondered why I felt the way I did. I certainly wasn't in love with this man I just met. I wasn't in love with Anni. It was a stunning shock to me that my body would react like this. My stomach fluttered with unrestrained want.

"Darling, you look like you've seen a ghost. Are you sure you are alright with this?" Anni said, coming into my vision. Her beautiful fingers tipped with lacquered nails as red as her lily when she bloomed, reached out, and touched the tips of my breasts gently. As much as I may try, I couldn't suppress the gasp that snuck from my lips.

"Yes," My voice moaned more than I was comfortable with, making her giggle.

"Oh, so you liked that did you?" She was a little more forceful this time, pinching my nipples so that lightning zipped through my body. "Kameron, be rough with her. I want to see what she can take."

I looked back at him, now naked, his cock much bigger than I imagined cocks being. For some reason, before now, I thought they were all relatively the same size. He slid his thighs up behind mine, pushing up against me intimately.

"Do you want that, Lenora?" His voice sang to me, "Do you want me to be rough with you?"

I didn't know what rough was like, but it sounded appealing. It sounded like the answer to my aching sex. Trembling, I opened my mouth and moaned. His cock sliding along my lily, rubbing right at the bud of my pleasure.

"A moan isn't consent, Lenora," Kameron said again. "I want to have you. I need you to tell me that is alright."

Was it alright? My mind swirled in the heat of him rubbing up against me, and I almost didn't answer. Was it okay to do this with someone other than Lukas? *Was this ever alright?* Heart thumping in my chest, I decided that it was acceptable because Lukas was gone forever, and I was never supposed to have him in the first place.

I took so long to answer that Kameron pulled away from me before I could breathe out, "Yes, please. Yes, take me."

The next thing I knew, he filled me. I moaned at the stretch.

"Damn, you're tight." His voice seemed a bit uneven. He thrust, and Anni swallowed my moan, pressing her pretty lips against mine as the world around me spun. He took a fast rough pace immediately, making me burn in my desire.

Anni abandoned kissing my lips in favor of squeezing one of my breasts while Kameron used the other to hold on tight.

"Ohhh." I gasped as the tempo of my heart increased. "I'm almost there."

"Cum for me," Kameron commanded, pushing in as deep as he could. I could feel him swirl his hips, causing the slosh in my pelvis to ignite.

"Yes." I cried out, "Oh yes!" And between the two of them, I lost myself to a blinding orgasm so powerful that I swore my heart was going to stop.

Kameron was still thrusting through my capitulation to bliss. As I could feel the heavy thudding pulse through all the parts of me, I heard him moan.

"Kameron, dear, pull out. She hasn't been given any contraceptives yet." Anni sang as I became aware of her helping him back. Her hand rubbing up and down his wet cock as his cum spurted out all over me.

I froze for a moment remembering Lukas cuming in me right before the world turned upside down. But there were no booms in the distance. The ocean was so far away it would never reach Elevar, and the only thing that happened was Anni giggled and kissed Kameron's cheek.

"Maybe I should leave her training in your hands."

I stayed still where they left me, heat quickly fading away from my skin. Kameron laughed at her words and leaned over me.

"How about it, Lenora? Would you like me to stay for a little while and train you? I doubt Lopuri's Arena is going to be holding shows anytime soon, so I don't have any other place to be."

I looked at him, confused.

"What do you have to do with the Arena?" He looked proud of himself at the question. As if he was showing off, he raised his arms and flexed his impressive muscles.

"I'm The Undefeated!"

And that was how I found out that the second man I made love with was one of my family's biggest foes.

Chapter Eight

THE FOLLOWING DAY WHEN Kameron requested me to join him for breakfast, I had Mama's voice swimming through my head. There were few things Mama told me about her days at the Arena, but one of them was about him; The Undefeated, who was ironically defeated only once.

"He's a horrible person." Mama's voice echoed in my head while Kameron sat across from me, stirring his Velox tea with one of Elevar's silver spoons. I sipped my tea, wondering why Mama would have had such a bad feeling about Kameron? But it wasn't just her; Papa came home swearing every year after The Undefeated took out the house's lead fighter. I remembered hearing Lukas and Jonathan say that the man was a monster to behold.

That seemed silly. Kameron was no monster, just a tall man with a fighter's physique. Skin like the night sky and a storm melded into him in the most perfect, awe-inspiring way.

"You seem distracted, Lenora." The way he said my name reminded me of having sex with him. Indeed, that wasn't horrible, but what about him might be? I blushed and put my teacup down.

"I'm sorry. I was thinking about my family." I knew how it sounded, sad and wistful. He didn't realize that it wasn't, that I was just trying to pick apart inconsistencies of experience and hearsay.

Kameron leaned heavily on the table, "I heard from Ava about what your father did to you. Real men don't drop their children into slavery when they have problems." His voice sounded bitter as if he took personal offense to my treatment. It made me blush more.

"I- I'm not enslaved," My stutter was defensive, and for a moment, I saw a look cross his face that I didn't like. It was a heartbreak, his brow wrinkled, and his eyes grew soft. Even the beautiful marks on his cheeks seemed to dull.

"If you aren't, then you would have other options than being here, and I doubt any of the girls here would have stayed if there were options available to them."

I didn't argue with that. My decision to stay here was rooted in having a roof over my head and food to eat. I knew I would never make it on my own, but I didn't think it was the same as slavery, and I pushed my morning bread around my plate, trying to think of a way to express that to him.

"It's still a choice to be here," I replied.

"That's what all you girls say," He huffed before taking an agitated sip of his tea. "You can't tell me you love being required to spread your legs for any man who pays and picks you. And if you don't, there are dire consequences. That's why I call it slavery. No matter how nice Ava is to you, she is your master telling you who to sleep with, when, and how or you face almost certain death."

I didn't want to talk about those truths. They still hurt. They still ripped open my heart and made me terrified. Nervously I fumbled with my teacup. My fingers were shaking, and not for the first time a wave of homesickness washed through me. The sea, as much as it terrified me, was a staple in my life. I couldn't remember ever having spent this long away from it.

My silence must have been too long because the next thing I knew, Kameron had reached out and grabbed my hand.

"I'm sorry," He whispered, "These things must still be tough for you, and I'm not judging your decision to stay. I just feel enraged that this is the only option for you and the rest of the fine women here."

I paused before whispering back, "Why do you care so much? I'm not stupid; I know that other men might not act like you in taking me. You act like you're in love when you don't even know who I am."

He didn't answer. I wasn't sure if I expected him to because my question was more personal than we were close. Instead, his marks lit up briefly incandescent across his face. Then he drank down the rest of his chalky Velox tea.

"Since your training lays with me now, I figured we could start with some basics," his tone begged for attention. "The men you meet here will want whatever services you are willing to give, and some you aren't willing to give."

I closed my mouth nervously and watched as he put both his elbows on the table. Clearly unmannered, he propped his head up in his hands.

"What aren't you willing to do?" He asked, and my mind went blank.

"I- I don't know."

"Are you willing to call a man your master?" He growled the words as if they deeply displeased him, "Are you willing to crawl on your hands and knees for him? Are you willing to handle excrement? Are you willing to let him bleed you?"

I shivered, and not in a good way. None of those things sounded fun.

"I suppose I have to be if the client wants that."

"No." Kameron slammed his hand down on the table, startling me. "You get a say in what you do. If you are uncomfortable with something, you can kick any man out even if they offer more money."

I was uncomfortable with this conversation. My insides felt like jelly, and the meek part of me shrunk back. I must have physically pulled back to because that was the next thing Kameron commented on.

"Are you afraid of me?"

"No. I'm overwhelmed by you." I breathed out and watched him stand from the table. He took a few quick strides around to where I sat and leaned up against the lip. I half wondered if I should tell him to be careful of my teacup. When I didn't, he overturned it with his hip, and the golden tea spilled all down the side of his pants.

"Ausur's Grace," He mumbled to himself but glanced back at me. "Lenora, you are so innocent. I could see it in your eyes when I thrust myself in your lily. You don't know how to stand up for yourself, which is the biggest lesson you need to learn here in Elevar. If you don't, men will take advantage of you, and women will take advantage of you. Don't be fooled into thinking the other girls up here won't cut your throat to get more money." He leaned over, sliding his hand along my cheek, "They will. Even my sweet Anni could be ruthless if she felt you were competition."

His rough fingers were sliding along my jaw, tickling me down my throat. The touch was intimate and personal, but so were his words. I didn't know if I should trust him, but I suspected he was right about what would happen to me if I didn't toughen up. That was what Mama had to do, after all. Toughen up and become the first woman in Lopuri's Arena or die as a whore in the streets. I felt ashamed that I put myself in a position she had fought her way out of.

Then, I got an idea. I looked up to Kameron's dark eyes and met his gaze.

"Teach me how to fight." That got him laughing, loud and strong. But I was serious. I reached up and grabbed his shirt by the front. Digging my fingers in, I repeated myself. "Kameron, The Undefeated, teach me how to fight."

I was not amused when he leaned over and kissed my forehead as if everything I said was adorable.

"Women don't fight." He finally sobered. Except I knew he was lying.

"Yes, they do. There was a famous woman who fought you in Diss. I've heard there is a book about it. And..." I stuttered and knew I was going to confide in him. I would tell him this personal thing, and it might change how he looked at me, but I had to try. "And you lost to my mother in Lopuri."

I couldn't have predicted the befuddled look on his face as he processed my words. His lips moved in a mimicry of what I said, and then he grabbed me.

"Your mother is Julia!"

"Yes," I affirmed, "She was before the sea took her away from me. And I am just as capable of fighting as she was."

Kameron laughed this time softer, with a bit of sadness to his voice.

"You know, I can see her in your face now. I'm so sorry she died."

It was silent for a few minutes, me taking in the sound of not-hate from Kameron's voice. It was strange. I thought that he would have hated her as much as she told her children she hated him. I wondered what had happened between them.

Kameron stood up from the dining table and walked a few paces towards the big ballroom of Elevar before turning to me.

"If you want me to teach you to fight, you better come along."

I scrambled along after him ignoring the mess of our breakfast table for the prospect of learning to be on my own. Briefly, I imagined that this training would allow me to break free and become independent. I knew I couldn't go back home, but maybe I could travel to the northern city of Diss and fight in their Arena for a living. Perhaps I could go out to the rocky ocean port of Moorelend and live there. I didn't have to be a whore! I could find value in myself.

The ballroom for Elevar was gigantic, with beautiful marble and gold-plated floors, high ceilings, and plenty of space.

Completely unmannered Kameron yanked his shoes and socks off in the middle of the floor, throwing them off to the side.

"Bare feet in here, Lenora," He said to my aghast gaze, "Your shoes will make you slip all over this dancefloor."

Hesitantly I lifted one leg, unlacing my boot, tossing it, feeling the cold marble rush up my ankle and into my toes as I placed it back down. Kameron saw through my hesitation and grinned widely.

"You told me you wanted to learn how to fight! Now take off that other shoe and fight me." I scrambled to do just that when he rushed me. I gaped at his speed. He ran so fast my eyes could barely keep up with him, and while I struggled to unlace my second boot, he managed to unbutton the whole back of my gown. Unreal.

My face flushed, and I cried out, "That's not fair! We aren't having sex. You're teaching me how to fight!"

"And do you really think you can fight in a frilly gown?" Kameron laughed, "Even your mother fought in her underwear before she got the Arena to supply armor for her!"

I didn't know that, but his words had value. I shimmied out of the light blue gown, reminding myself that right now, everything I owned belonged to others. Right now, I was in debt, helpless, and Kameron had better provide me with a means not to be helpless any longer.

My dress came off. All I had was my underwear and my camisole so thin and see-through. I tried not to blush in embarrassment, realizing that this was how exposed Mama was when she first started fighting. I hoped with all my heart that Papa gave her armor and a place fast.

I stood looking at Kameron. He had put his hands to his hips and tossed his head to the side as if wondering something.

"What is it?" I asked, shaking with how exposed I was. The ballroom was cold compared to the more lived-in areas of the castle.

"I was just reminiscing how familiar this felt." He mused out loud and then shook his head, his black braids swimming through the movement. "Now come on, Lenora, you've got to have a fighting spirit in you. You got to show me you mean this."

I tried. I raised my arms, fists closed and squared my body off to Kameron the way I had seen Jonathan and Lukas play fight.

"You're so cute." He mumbled and then rushed forward, lightning-fast. I felt something; maybe his hand impacted my shoulder, not hard enough to bruise, but hard enough to push me back.

I stumbled and realized I lost sight of him. My heart was pounding. I couldn't help but dart my eyes around, feet tripping on the cold floor. I never actually saw him move. I just saw blurs, streaks of something fast around me. How was I supposed to win? How was I supposed to fight?

With a bit of anger in my heart, I realized that Kameron was just messing with me. He had no intention of teaching me how to fight at all. And that was why I decided he must be the one place I couldn't see. I was going to get him.

I swung my hands backward and surprised myself by catching wool in them. Immediately I kicked back, as hard as I could with my soft heal.

"Ow!" Kameron exclaimed, then pulled me down to the floor. Not sure what this meant, I kept lashing out, hitting his arms as they encircled me. "Oh, stop it. We are done. I know what I need to know to teach you how to fight."

"But we didn't do anything yet?" I was breathless on the ground, him over me. Dark eyes were traveling down my neck to my breasts.

"I determined that you are aware of your surroundings. You know where to look, and you aren't afraid to act. I think that is a win for the first day of training."

I flushed, looking up into his face, afraid to move, not wanting to.

"Then what are we doing now?" I whispered. Kameron just grinned, and I could see on the left side where he had lost two teeth to leave a gaping hole in his mouth.

"Your other training." He growled before kissing me. Oh, my mind stuttered to a stop, and I blabbered.

"Here? Anyone could walk in on us."

He shrugged while I panicked. Behind my eyes, I remembered the moment Lukas's door opened, and my world as I knew it ended. I tried to swallow the acidic bile on my tongue, but I couldn't quench the terrible heart-wrenching feeling that if someone were to walk in, it would be over again. Something worse would happen. Maybe the world would end.

I pushed Kameron off of me.

"Not here," Surprised to hear myself sob, "Not where people can walk in." I squeezed my eyes shut, trying to cut out the memory of water over my feet, of the sea, rising, of watching the red tones of it rumbling towards me.

Kameron didn't argue. He put his hand on my shoulder and patted it.

"I bothered you, didn't I?"

Struggling still, I debated whether to tell him. I still hadn't discovered what made him so unlikeable to my family, and I was pretty sure I liked him just fine. So I lifted my toes, looking at the cold pink of them.

"It's not about you." I wiped away my tears. "The first time I had sex was the day the Bloodstar died. Lukas and I snuck home past the evacuation zone to be together, and Papa and Mama found us. Then the sea took everything."

There was a rustling by my side. I looked over to see that Kameron had gotten to his feet.

"Let me bring you to your room, Lenora." I let him gather our stuff and expected my dress back, but he didn't readily give it. He looked at the chiffon and frowned, "I'm only allowed to be with you right now because Ava thinks that I'm training you to become a whore. I see now that you don't have that in your heart, but you still need to pretend you do until we can find some way out of this for you."

I agreed and tried to hold my head high, walking half-naked back to my room, but I noticed the eyes of several girls watching us through the halls. Kameron acted as if he didn't notice at all, though, and so I aspired to be as unflappable as he was. He saw me to my room like a gentleman and even hung up my dress for me.

I went and sat down on my bed, feeling shaky and dismayed. When Kameron turned around, he put his hands to his hips.

"What could I do to help you feel better?" He questioned as if my feelings were his responsibility. They weren't. We barely knew each other. I shrugged, and he came closer, bending at his tall waist to look me in the eye.

"Make this be a bad dream? Make me not have gone with Lukas?" I breathed out softly and wished that demons could turn back time. They didn't, of course, but they had other powers, and maybe that's why he sat on my bedside instead of leaving me to my misery.

"I can't make it never happen, but maybe... maybe I can make it hurt less." His words whispered in my ear, his breath tickled my hair. "But you have to tell me it's alright to do. Most humans don't like this."

"What is it?" I questioned curiously. I flushed at how close he was to me.

His lips slid along my cheek, dark over light. Out of the corner of my eye, I saw his marks light up again.

"I can possess you, walk you through some of the harder moments in your memory. It would let you look at it outside of the situation, and maybe that will help you heal."

He was right. I wasn't ready for that yet. Squirming a little, I turned and caught his lips with mine—an openmouthed kiss, so full of heat and promise. Vaguely I became aware that he had grabbed my wrists and was circling his thumbs over the pressure points in the middle.

I broke the kiss to whisper back to him.

"I appreciate the offer, but I'm not ready for that yet." Then I stuttered, "I- I am ready to make love to you though if you want."

He chuckled, "You don't have to ask me twice." He pushed me back on the bed and undressed me with care. He took the time to pull his fingers over my thighs, to scrape my knees with his fingers. It was gentle caresses that held firm my breath.

My whole body tingled when he pulled my legs wide.

"You- you still aren't undressed," I complained, finding it unfair that he could look upon me, but I couldn't in return. His fingers slid along the inside of my thighs.

"I think you need a reward for having managed to catch me in the ballroom." His voice was husky, and I was about to ask what reward he was talking about when he lowered his head between my legs. Shivering, I felt him lick me on the inside of my thigh first while his fingers gently rubbed my lily. Soft, sweet heat seeped into me. Rub, rub, rub, *lick*. It was blissful to feel his tongue sliding over my petals, swirling over the bud of my sex. I sighed and sighed again. Hot, oh, I was heating up so fast, itching to dig my fingers into something and hold on. First, it was the sheets I gripped, but he kept the pace slow and sensual, just enough to keep me going.

"Kameron," I moaned out his name when he finally molded his lips over me and sucked. It would have been impossible to stop, to resist the urge to wrap my hands through his thick braids, so I did. Holding on, he seemed even more enthusiastic. Licking hard, then soft, swirling his tongue over and over until I thought I'd die in the fire of it.

"Say my name again." He ordered, pulling back to slip two fingers into the space between my petals. They slid in and added pressure I craved.

"Kameron," I gasped. He started thrusting his fingers, wet because I was soaked, and the fire in my belly built.

"Louder."

"Kameron." I managed an even tone, and he rewarded me with a quick rub along my bud. I looked down to see him watching me, his marks alight and beautiful. He grinned.

"Scream it." The command was given just before he latched onto me and started sucking and rubbing with his tongue so hard my legs shook.

"Kameron!" My voice screamed to the ceiling, but inside, the fire consumed me. My lungs sucked for air, my legs shook until they were useless, and the deep pulse of satisfaction filled my chest.

I didn't know how long I was staring at the ceiling, but eventually, Kameron pulled me up.

"I guess I owe you a new blanket." He laughed, and I didn't know why until a moment later when I looked and found the only blanket on my bed drenched from my passion. Still swimming in post bliss, I let him make me stand.

"What about you?"

He tossed my blanket on the floor and then pushed me back on the bed. I was honestly perplexed when he crawled over me to lay by my side.

"That was good enough for me." He said when I looked at him with confusion. "I wanted to make you feel better, and I did. Now how about we take a nap before the twins start their evening performance?"

Kameron fell asleep in my bed, but I couldn't help and watch him wondering how it was that he was willing to please me without getting anything in return? That hadn't been my experience before. Any gifts I received from Lukas were laden with the promise that I would somehow be good for him. What made this man different? What made my family hate him?

I thought maybe I'd have these questions forever.

Chapter Nine

MY BARE FEET HIT the marble floor, and I took off running. It was as fast as I could go, as fast as I was able, but that didn't matter in the face of Kameron's preternatural speed. He zoomed by me with ease and waited for me at the end of the ballroom, grinning wide.

"You're not bad for a human," he said when I finally got to the end. "But I bet we can get you even faster with practice!"

"And what does this have to do with her training?" Anni questioned, walking up to us from where she had been watching since we began this day—running training because Kameron insisted that sometimes the best course of action was simply to run away. It didn't look like Anni agreed because the proper Rathinian whore couldn't even contain her frown behind the black silk fan she held up to her face.

"Ah, Anni, don't worry! There's more than one way to train." Kameron said, but it was a little bit of a lie since Kameron, and I already determined that this training was to get me out of here. To give me the means to make money more reputably, with something I was willing to do.

"And how is running related to sex, Kameron?" Anni questioned sourly, "I permitted you to train her so that I could have more free time. I've reduced my client load so that you can get this right. Instead, I'm making debts and losing money to Ava!"

That got Kameron's attention. I watched him take on a concerned look and reach out to her.

"What debts are you taking on? Do you need help?" Kameron asked seriously. Anni snapped down her fan quickly, and I could see the flushing scowl on her face.

"I needed new moon rags; they cost almost 40 coin apiece. And on top of that, my monthly allotment of Alphita tea, soap supply, and a new dress, it's more than 560 coins for my monthly debt!" She moaned, clearly aggravated by the situation.

"Why do moon rags cost so much?" I asked her, stunned, "In Lopuri, they are half that!"

"Because, Lenora, Ava controls all the products that come in and out of Elevar. One of your lessons needs to be in budgeting and frugalness, or you'll be owing more than you can pay off in a season." Anni replied.

"What happens then?"

"That's when you become a slave and have to sleep with men that you don't want to sleep with," Kameron grumbled. "Ava thinks she's so progressive having gotten rid of sales costs for you girls, but she's just as bad as her predecessor because she's put that cost in other places."

"Nothing is ever free, Kameron, despite your ideals." Anni reprimanded softly, her pretty hands patting down the backs of his big ones.

Those words made me worry for a moment. I had been given everything I needed since I came to Elevar, with no mention, not even a peep about what I owed. I had hand-me-down gowns from Marie and Anni, the twins gave me soap, I didn't have moon rags yet, but right now, that wasn't a problem.

My fingers twitched.

"Where does that lead me? I've been here almost three weeks, and I haven't paid for anything yet."

Anni reached out and grabbed my hands, patting them softly. She was so calm and centered, so soft and reserved.

"Don't worry about it yet, Lenora. My sisters and I have been giving you the things you need. Room and board are always free for us ladies, but you will need to speak with Ava about buying moon rags and Alphita tea very soon. Birthing babies is an expense in Lopuri, and if you were to have a girl, she'd end up like me."

I didn't have to hear what the 'like me' meant. I knew. Anni stayed because she was born here. A whole lifetime of debts to Elevar.

Instead of acknowledging it, I stammered, "I-I have been using a lucky penny when I'm with Kameron. Is that enough?"

"It's always better to do both." Anni replied, "Three years ago, Marie got pregnant using just Alphita tea. She was lucky the baby was a boy and able to be adopted out, but she still owes from the birth cost."

I looked at Kameron and knew my face had paled badly. He just moved from one foot to the other uncomfortably before speaking again.

"Anni, maybe you should go over the cost of items and budgeting with Lenora. I know how to handle money on the outside, but here there are a lot of hidden costs, and you'll know better where they are than I would."

"Some other time," Anni waved us off. "I have a special request client coming in an hour."

Horrified, I blushed and was almost too embarrassed to ask, but I did because I needed to know. "You have to take clients when you are on your moon blood?" *That was a sacred time for a woman's body!*

Anni giggled a little and flushed herself.

"Oh, Kameron, that should be your next training. Teaching her how to please a man when she is on her moon blood is a top priority, and you'd like that, wouldn't you, my demon?"

The flirty way she spoke with him threw me off because I was still so caught up in being embarrassed, and so did his deep laugh.

"I would indeed."

Standing there unmoving, I simply looked between the two of them as Anni said her goodbyes with a giggle and leaned up to kiss Kameron's cheek. I was curious about her words and curious about them. Was I getting between them?

I shook my head of those thoughts when Kameron came back to me, grinning from ear to ear. Again I noticed the hole in his smile where teeth were missing.

"I think we can stop with running for the day," Kameron growled in the sexiest way I ever heard a man speaking, "Why don't we retire somewhere else where I can show you how to please a man during your moon blood."

I hesitated, and he noticed.

"Why would a man even want to have sex when I'm bleeding?" I asked, "Wouldn't it get everywhere?" Even with moon rags, it sometimes got everywhere. I wrinkled my nose, remembering that I had accidentally bled through on my nightgown during my last moon blood. I remembered the sticky wet feeling of it on my butt and Mama scolding me to remember to sleep on my side rather than my back.

Kameron shrugged, "Sometimes it's messy. And it's not as bad as you are thinking. Come with me, and I'll show you."

I still didn't understand how he would show me when I was not currently bleeding, but I went along with him anyway, away from the ballroom, up a floor away from my room to a series of rooms I had not seen before.

He clicked open the door to the first one, and I stepped into a bathing room I had previously been unaware existed.

"Come on, let's take a bath together." His voice rumbled in my ears, and I flushed. Typically baths were separated by gender, though I did hear salacious rumors saying they weren't in the north. And Kameron did come from the north.

Hot-faced, I nodded. I went to prepare the bath, but Kameron was ahead of me, turning on the taps to one of the three large tubs in the room.

"Why do you keep training me in sex when you are also training me to fight?" I asked after Kameron shut the tap off, and the sound quieted again. Kameron unbuttoned his shirt.

"Mostly because sex is fun. I like having it with you, and I hope you'll continue to want it with me. Nothing else."

I looked back to the bathtub.

"So sex in a tub?" I asked.

"Well, some men might like that, but I don't. It's too slippery and somehow less enjoyable." Kameron made a face of distaste, "We're just having a bath together to relax, and then I'll tell you about what we are going to do."

I didn't entirely trust him, but I got undressed and entered the bath's warm water anyway. Immediately he was by my side, smoothing his hands over my skin, playing with my breasts in the water.

"I thought you were going to talk to me?" I giggled when he accidentally tickled my arm.

"I am," He pulled away only a little, only enough to wrap his muscular arm around my shoulders. The warmth of his skin seeped into mine. "One thing you can do when you are on your moon blood is have sex with a man in a tub like this one with your lucky penny in your lily. It should keep too much blood from seeping out, and the little bit that does will go away in the water."

"But you said you don't like having sex in the water." I pointed out softly.

"I don't. I'm just giving you options in case..."

"I don't want to stay," I affirmed. "I want to go fight in one of the Arena's, like my mother before me."

Kameron was quiet for a second, and I couldn't tell if I had said something wrong or not. Worried that I may have, I reached out and touched his knee.

"You could do this." He moved on, grabbing my hand and bringing it to his half-hard cock. Wrapping our fingers around the thick base, he started sliding my hand up and down at a pace that made my cheeks blush. "Most men don't mind this." He whispered lustily, "But there are even better options."

The water around me sloshed with movement, and I realized he had lifted himself to sit on the flat side of the tub. I could see the amorous way he held himself from here. His hands were mimicking what he just had me do.

"Would a man be willing to watch me and help himself?" I guessed and felt a little silly when I rubbed my hands down my breasts. I didn't feel like I had enough experience to pull off, making it look sexy, but he moaned anyway and pulled his hand away from his standing cock.

"Some might, but what I'd like is for you to use your mouth."

I was thoroughly perplexed, intrigued, and filled with wanting. Kameron being excited aroused me. When he motioned me forward, I came like a loyal puppy. He reached out, his calloused hands teasing my lips. Fingertips left my skin, replaced by the soft skin of his cockhead. I looked up to him, confused, feeling the softness of it brushing back and forth.

He didn't provide any more instruction, so I sought to ask him, but when I opened my mouth, he slid in, letting me taste the skin's neutral flavor—lips over him, my tongue along the underside of his slit. I remembered how he licked me in bed and thought to do much the same to him.

One short lick, he moaned.

Two a longer trek up to his length, he said my name.

Three, four, five, this new way to please him caught my curiosity. His gasps and wiggles made me feel proud, made my skin flush. I wanted this. I wanted him.

One more, and I got brave, taking as much of his strong cock in my mouth as I could, swirling my tongue from side to side in anticipatory delight.

"I'm going to cum." He growled out, "Damn gods, Lenora, you've got me going fast." I didn't stop to wonder what would happen when he did cum. Instead, his words emboldened me, made me lick him faster, and swallow him deeper. It occurred to me that his testicles were squeezing up closer to his body, and I lifted one hand to smooth my fingers over their surface, to cup them in my palm, and bravely touch him in a way I never had before.

He stopped making sounds at the moment, almost like his breath was stolen by my lips. Then I felt it gushing over my tongue. A little salty and tart, surprising. Fire zipped into my belly when I realized I just made him cum. Me, not his actions to me, but me! I caused this, and then I had to let go because the liquid in my mouth was getting too much, and I didn't know what to make of it.

As soon as I let his cock free, he grabbed my face in his strong hands.

"Let me see my cum in your mouth." The order was bliss-filled, growly, and low. His pupils dilated, deep black, and his demon marks splashing light into the darkness of his skin. I opened my mouth obediently and heard him laugh low. "Another lesson, if you were ever to do this with someone else, some men want you to swallow their seed. I don't care, whatever makes you most comfortable."

He let me go, and I closed my mouth, swallowing down the cooling sort of sticky liquid.

"I liked that," I confessed with a blush. "I like making you cum."

He laughed, all white teeth and a wide smile.

"Good thing, I like it too." He slid back into the tub, "But we should bathe and then go to dinner together. Later on tonight, I'll show you another way to please me when you are bleeding, though honestly, the blood doesn't bother me."

He put his arm around me, and my mind swam with nervous glee.

"You said please you, not other men." I pointed out. He dumped a cup of water over my head, and I didn't know what to think when he neglected to acknowledge my words. Could we be a couple? When I escaped and went to the Arena to fight, could I travel with him? Could I fight by his side?

While he washed my hair, I looked at the ceiling and imagined talking to Mama in the stars. *Why did you hate Kameron? He's an amazing man. He's everything I could ever want, and I trust him.*

But the stars were silent, and Mama's voice was absent from my head.

Chapter Ten

HE FLIRTED WITH ME all dinner, even when Anni showed up after servicing her special request client. I noticed that she watched us from the other side of the table where Marie counted the number of chilies she could eat on a dare from the twins. Her pretty eyes kept glancing over to Kameron, to me. And it made me uncomfortable, nervous even.

Am I getting in their way?

I couldn't help but wonder because the twins liked to talk loudly about how Kameron was always Anni's. Every season when he passed through Elevar, all he did was for Anni.

And now, I was in the picture. Awkwardly, stuck there where I didn't really belong because if life happened the way it was supposed to, I'd still be with my family, and that dreadful day when the Bloodstar died wouldn't have happened.

"So, did you find out anything about Lopuri from your client?" Ava asked Anni loudly, clearly trying to catch her attention. Everyone quieted for a moment, and Anni nodded.

"Yes, apparently Lopuri is going to host a royal wedding between the Katharos and the Rathinians," Anni exclaimed. "Ausur knows why they are doing that!"

"Back to business as usual then," Kameron muttered. "That's surprising. I was in Diss when the Bloodstar fell into the moon. The city is wrecked."

"You were in Diss? It takes a month to get there." Bella scoffed, handing a glass of water to Marie, who looked like she had eaten one pepper too many, "I don't believe you."

I did, but only because I had seen how fast Kameron could run. If he ran straight here from the northern capital... well, I didn't doubt he could do it in the time it took for us to be introduced.

"Well, I didn't exactly want to stick around and wait for them to start blaming demons," Kameron grumbled to her.

"Is there any other news? How did he say the city was fairing?" Ava pressed, and I thought I knew why. Lopuri was the closest city to Elevar. The majority of clients probably went through my home city before coming here. If things were so bad that tourism suffered, so would the fortunes of the ladies of the mountain.

Anni shrugged, "There wasn't much talking."

Marie snorted, and I couldn't tell if it was in response to the tiny red pepper she chewed on or to be rude to Anni's words.

"You shortsighted girl." Ava scolded, "You know to gather information when we can. Oh, this whole thing has me worried about a hike in prices." Ava wrung her hands, but from where I was sitting, it looked more like she was delighted at the prospect of charging girls and customers alike extra. It made me uneasy.

I wasn't the only one put off by the sight. Next to me, Kameron cleared his throat and leaned into the table.

"Anni, could I borrow your kit tonight?"

Kit? My curiosity bubbled up inside me. What kit? What was he planning? Across from us, Anni giggled and leaned in.

"You're planning on using the kit? I want to be there, otherwise no deal."

"You know you are always welcome, Anni, my beautiful princess." Kameron crooned even though Ava made a sound of disgust. He answered nothing for me, and it didn't look like it would be anytime soon. When we finished up with our food, it was off to chores. Today was my day for laundry, the one task even more physically demanding than flushing the toilets.

I was achy and up to my armpits in scrubbing water when Kameron showed up.

"Do you want some help?"

I looked at him sideways and wrinkled my brow.

"Why do you want to help? Don't you have anything else to do?"

"Well, no, I'm a client, Ava doesn't usually give me chores, and Anni's job today was dusting. I finished that for her an hour ago." His explanation had me frowning, wondering, just like I wondered this morning. Was I getting between them? He helped her first. He only came to me now because he was bored.

Still, I didn't say anything. I just scooted over and let Kameron take a place next to me. I wasn't going to argue help with the laundry. He sat down next to me.

"Oh, you have bedsheets today?" He stuck his hands in the water, iridescent soap bubbles climbing up the dark of his arms.

"Only five rooms worth," I chirped as cheerfully as I could. "Ava said we had a few visitors in the last few days. I never even saw them."

Kameron nodded, "I was aware of three. They came as a group two nights ago for trade from Scir. I don't think they saw any of the girls. It was just a business trip."

I nodded and tried to scrub out a particularly tough stain in the wet material I had.

"Ava told me that is common."

Kameron nodded and helped me hang up the wet sheet in the back of the room. As soon as I hung the material up, dripping down to the drains, Kameron had me in his arms. I didn't mind it at all when he leaned in and kissed me, tongue sliding along mine.

When he let go, I was dizzy and fluttery, my head swimming with loving thoughts. *Stop it,* I said to myself with ever dying emphasis; he *doesn't love me. He's just a client.*

"Lenora," He sang my name and made my thoughts seem dishonest, "Here, take this." He dug into his pocket and pulled out a pill. Freshly pressed, it looked a tinge green, and maybe mossy?

I picked it up between my fingers.

"What is it for?"

"It's to help prepare you for tonight." He laughed a little, "I am sorry, it's not going to feel pleasant."

Dubiously I looked at him, then back to the pill. Why would he want me to take something that was going to be unpleasant? Why should I agree?

"Why should I do this?" I echoed. He leaned in and kissed me again, mouth searching, hands over my breasts, squeezing. Again the dizzy rush of lust washed over my brain. I wished he would just take me on the floor of the washroom.

"I'm just teaching you something else," He swore, "I promise I'll make it worth your temporary upset. Trust me."

I did. I trusted Kameron and took the green pill that he handed me, anticipating that he would make the whole world feel right. He would make me feel amazing. He stayed by me and helped me finish the laundry, which was good because the first thing that happened was I started seeing color climb up the wall. My head was dizzy, my mouth dry. The world seemed fluid in a way that it hadn't before, slipping and sliding over itself. And my skin burned where he touched me.

"Take me," I begged him even though my vision was unsteady, my voice echoed in my ears, everything wobbled and wavered. And all I wanted was his cock pounding in me. I needed it, or I was surely going to die.

"I promise I will later." He swore right before I started cramping. At first, I thought it was my moon blood coming to ruin the night, but Kameron seemed to know I would feel this way. High, crampy, awful, and elated at the same time. He brought me to the bathrooms, where I got sicker than I had ever been before. High and hunched over with my body raging.

At least the color was still slinking up the wall like little snakes. At least his hands holding me steady still felt like delicious fire.

I was sure I blacked out because I was in Anni's room when I opened my eyes—laying naked on her bed, my skin tingling. Leftover traces of the drug Kameron gave me made her sheets feel like silk, made the ceiling look like water, and made the sound of her moaning feel like a song. I sat up, searching for them.

They were at the foot of the bed. Kameron brought his hand down and slapped Anni's bottom, jiggling the flesh there.

"Good good, Anni." He was saying in the same sexy growl he used with me. I flushed when his fingers dipped into her lily and pumped. My breath caught in my chest, and everything wiggled in the room before I noticed that she had something square on her. Right above her lily. I wondered what it was.

"Oh!" Kameron exclaimed. "Look who's woken up! Come on, Anni, let's get Lenora ready." He sounded so jovial like this was a game. I watched Anni crawl from her spot on the floor, like a sleek jungle cat, coming up to the bed to get me. I half expected her to pounce.

"Hmm, you're a little high still, aren't you?" She purred and leaned down, licking me from my jaw up to my cheek. Yes, dizzy, yes, colors moved weird. And dead gods, I wanted sex as if I would die if I didn't have it. Insatiable, hungry.

"Take me," I mumbled, a little lost in the feelings, hyperaware when Kameron grabbed my ear in his teeth and nibbled. It sent shock after tremendous shock of heat straight to my sex. Anni pulled my legs wide and slid her fingers up my lily, strumming back and forth over my bud, driving me insane. Hot, hot, hot, and the best was yet to come. Gasping, grabbing, sliding, I became aware of Kameron holding something small out of a nearby box. Something egg-shaped with a handle attached to the end.

"This is the smallest one Anni has," He said to me, showing off the object. "Now, don't be afraid. I'm going to put it in your ass." I must have looked at him like he was crazy because he laughed lowly, "I promise you'll like it, and if you don't, I'll take it out, and we won't use it again."

Heart pounding, I was still swimming in my head when Anni pulled my bottom, showing off my tight ass. I was swimming and filled with sensation when Kameron squeezed sweet oil all over me and then started to press. I gasped when it filled me up, slipping in easy, driving the fire deeper.

"What do you think, Lenora?" Anni whispered in my ear, "Makes you feel more, doesn't it?"

She was right. More different. Still filled with love and desire, I realized that the square I had seen on her was the handle of another one.

"Kiss me." She whispered and laid over me, breast to breast, hip to hip. We pressed our pelvis' together in the dark of her room. Without hesitation, I did what she asked—kissing, sucking her lips, enjoying the tender love of her.

Kameron loomed over us for a moment, and then I knew he shoved his cock straight into her lily when she started moving over me. I lost my breath and longed that I was her, secret thoughts still stimming through my brain.

He seems to really like her.

But if I thought I was simply trapped under them undulating over me, I was wrong. A moment later, Kameron switched to me. With the device inside of me, his cock hit me differently, filled me fuller than it had before. Breathtaking, and then he thrust, I moaned, and the world spun into the strings of pleasure and passion. Kameron switched back and forth between Anni and me.

I came fast, then came again. The dizzy high of the drug and the motion of our entangled bodies brought me to heights I couldn't even imagine. Anni laughed and kissed me; Kameron groaned and released his seed inside me. And all the moments thereafter were lost in darkness as I succumbed to the effervescent feelings washing over my soul.

104

Chapter Eleven

WE HAD BREAKFAST BROUGHT to us in Anni's room. Eggs and oats, with a massive pile of ham to mix with them. I poked at mine, not sure if I was hungry after last night.

"Rod root and Velox powder can make one lose their appetite for a few days," Anni said kindly from where she was sitting across the room. Her hands were hard at work, washing all of Kameron's dark curly hair. When I woke up, he had already taken it all out of the braids, and Anni immediately offered to wash it for him using expensive soap and a bowl of warm water.

I pushed away from the food and gathered my legs to me, hugging my knees.

"That's what you gave me? Rod root? I thought only men took it."

Kameron shrugged, "No, the drug works the same in women and men. The best aphrodisiac in the whole world makes for some interesting hallucinations."

I figured the Velox powder was what made me sick. Only a little was used in tea and drinking more than a few cups often led to stomach troubles. But now I understood why Kameron had employed it. I flushed, remembering what we did last night. I picked at the silver anklet that had shown up on me at some point in the night. I wondered what else we did that I couldn't remember.

I wondered why Anni groomed Kameron as if she did it every day of her life?

"Lenora, you look sad. What's wrong?" Anni asked. I startled out of my musings and blushed.

"I-I'm not sad!" I protested, but both of them were looking at me now.

"Well, alright." Anni said and rinsed out Kameron's hair, "You should find something relaxing to do today. Maybe read a book, or if you like to paint, Clara sometimes will share her paint set."

"Don't I have chores today?" I asked curiously. A day off? That wasn't usual from what I had seen. There was always something to be doing in Elevar.

"I paid for you to have a day to recover," Kameron said proudly, "I'll be doing your chores for today!"

Stunned, I just looked at him as Anni started parting his hair to rebraid it. He couldn't possibly do both of our chores for the day, no matter how fast he was. Which meant he chose to do mine and not hers.

"Thank you," I responded, not sure how to react. Anni looked up from the first tight braid, and I wondered how she knew how to do that? I wouldn't intuitively know how to braid his hair. The braids I knew worked best with straight hair, not the wild curls he had. *She must have done this for him before. Where do I stand? Am I just a whore?*

I teetered for a moment in my self-doubt and then slid off the bed.

"Thank you both. I'm going to go to my room and read, as you said. It seems like today is the best day for that."

Hurriedly I didn't give them a moment to say anything else. I grabbed my dress and rushed out of Anni's room. Thankfully no one was in the hallway, where I quickly pulled the blue material over my head and let it drop to my bare feet.

"What am I doing?" Hearing those words out loud made me even more uneasy. My stomach churned, and I sought the bathroom quickly.

After I finished vomiting the rest of the rod root and Velox out of my stomach, I made my way back to my room and shut myself inside. My heart raced, my eyes watered, and I clenched my fists against the door.

"I wish Mama was here," The tears came pouring down, over my cheeks, into the hollow of my throat. But Mama wasn't here. It was just me, alone, with no family and friends I didn't know if I could trust.

It was exhausting, and even though I tried to take my mind off it by reading, I was too tired. My eyes slipped closed with the book over my chest, and I dreamed.

In my dreams, I was standing on the Arena floor in my underwear. The crowds jeered at me screamed that a woman shouldn't be fighting. And still, I stood rooted by something deep within me, waiting to see what opponent would come out of the doors. Except it was nothing, I could fight. It was the sea, tinged red, roaring, raging, and I still couldn't move. I stood still as death as it covered my head, drowning me slowly until I screamed bubbles passing up through my lips as the world of water swallowed all the sound.

Just when I thought all hope was lost, he reached down, dark arms stretching through the waves, circling me, tugging me up.

"Wake up!" His voice yelled down to me. "Wake up!"

I tried to open my eyes. *Wake up? This must be a dream!* And with that realization, I gasped for breath, deep wheezy, only to find that vomit filled my mouth. Sour and acidic. I scrambled to get out of the water, but there was no longer water around me. The sea had receded, disappeared for my bed and the bitter stench of vomit.

The dream disappeared to reveal Kameron and Anni looking down worriedly at me. I sat up as quickly as I could, scared, startled, wondering how I could have vomited in my sleep and not have noticed it?

"Lenora, are you alright?" Kameron asked as if he was afraid I wasn't. Maybe I wasn't because I burst into tears and started trying to explain my dream. Drowning in the sea, except now I was in the Arena on top of it. Exposed, hurt, destined to die.

"Oh, poor girl," Anni pulled me off of the bed, making me stand on shaky legs, "We must have made the pill too strong. I'm so so sorry." She wiped away my tears, and behind me, I could hear Kameron stripping the bed down, balling up the soiled sheets and covers.

I was shaking and still.

"Anni, could you bring her bedding to be laundered? I am going to talk to her for a moment." Kameron said and pulled me back to the bare bed. Anni nodded and picked up my dirty, smelly things taking the stench of my sickness out of the room with her.

My shoulders were tense, and I wrung my hands.

"You're having bad dreams about what happened to you?" Kameron asked.

"Yes," I whispered, "Almost every night."

"You should let me possess you," He said softly, "I can bring you through your memories, walk you through them and make them less harmful."

I shook my head negatively, "Am I getting in between you and Anni?" I blurted out the question instead of taking up his offer. It jarred him; I could tell, almost feeling the sudden tenseness in his grip around my waist.

"No. No, you are not." He reached out to touch my hand, "Anni is my friend, but she is in love with another man, not me."

My breath held, and I looked at him.

"Who is she in love with?"

"A Rathinian who comes here to see her. He's tried to buy her and bring her to Haliban, where he lives, but Ava said her price was higher than he could afford. He hasn't been back since." Kameron said softly. "Anni is my friend. Why were you worried about that?"

My heart raced, and I realized I'd have to confess it. My secret thoughts, my secret feelings. My fragile heart. But I wanted to face Kameron as if I was a warrior and not some scared girl who thought her only lot in life was to be a whore. So I looked at him, His beautiful face, just a little bit of dark stubble over his chin, his demon marks alight and glowing. The light of them reflected in his eyes and made them glow.

"I like you." I whispered and watched his grin grow, then nervously, I repeated it, "I like you tremendously."

Leaning in, he hoisted me onto his lap, and then he spoke directly in my ear, so quiet, almost like he was afraid of anyone else hearing it.

"I like you, too." Then he chuckled, "I guess I didn't do a good job training you after all. We aren't supposed to like each other. We're only supposed to fuck."

"I want to read books with you," I responded, "I want to see you fight in the Arena. I want to cheer for you and then have you cheer for me when it's my turn."

He kissed me sweetly. I loved it.

"We need to get serious about your training then. You aren't ready to fight in the Arena yet. And we need to figure out a way to get you out of here. Anni's paramore was fairly wealthy, maybe more than I am. Ava probably will raise the price on you too."

"You're wealthy?" I giggled. It didn't matter much to me if he was or not, but he shrugged.

"I have some money saved. In case of emergencies." I didn't ask what emergencies he might face. I listened to him sigh and felt his arms around me, "You should go back to sleep.

I'll watch you this time. In case you get sick again. Tomorrow we train. Outside, so no one can guess what we are up to."

I agreed with him and looked forward to the day when I could show him that all his hard work was worth it.

Chapter Twelve

KAMERON'S COCK WAS POUNDING into me. Hard. Hot. Desirable, but all I could think of was the snow icing up my hands and knees and my breath puffing up in front of my face. The steam of it kept getting pushed back by the occasional wind outside Elevar, and that was making my face feel wet, which was uncomfortable. I didn't think I would cum this time, even though I wanted to.

I yearned for it in my gut and tried moaning louder than the wind in hopes that I could vocalize my way into bliss. I was ready to resign myself when he sped up, faster than he ever fucked me, a throbbing thrumming feeling right where I needed it. Promptly I orgasmed, my wetness squirting out into the snow between my knees. A moment later, he groaned and held himself as deep as he could go.

For a moment, we stayed that way, breathless in bliss, covered in snow.

It got cold fast in the snow. Kameron seemed to think so, too, because he pulled me up quickly.

"Ready to go back?" He asked with a smile. Teeth chattering, I nodded. "Alright, try to punch me. One last time."

"Kameron," I complained, but he crossed his arms in a fighting stance, and I knew he wasn't going to let me not do this. We had been doing this all morning. At dawn, he woke up determined that I needed to know how to punch—decided that throwing a fist with accuracy was the key to developing me into a good fighter.

I moaned and groaned about it. My arms were weak. My legs were strong. Couldn't I just kick him? No, punching first. So together, we went out into the snowy world outside of Elevar and trained.

I balled up my freezing fists and tried one last time to hit him where it counts. My hands felt weak, another gust of wind blew up my dress, and I got him. Right in the chest because he let me.

"Ow!" I exclaimed and pulled back my hand, "What?"

"Good job. That one probably broke a finger." He grabbed my painted hand, ripping off my glove to inspect my fingers.

"How is that good?!" I raised my voice incredulously. He shot me a dark glance before pulling the glove on my hand.

"It's good because you won't go in at an angle like that again." He said wisely, "Now come on. It's freezing out here, and I have some things to do tonight."

I followed him curiously at that and only spoke once we were inside the warmth of the castle.

"You aren't spending the night with me?" I tried not to sound whiny when I said it. As if he owed me that favor. I found myself loving it when he smiled.

"Sorry, Lenora, Ava said if I'm going to stay here, I have to help out. Especially since I'm not paying you for services rendered."

I flushed at the way he said it and also felt a little hurt. I hadn't had sex with him every day for two weeks because it was my job too. I was doing it because... my mind paused. Because he was nice to me? Because I was growing to love his imperfect smile? Because at night I pretended we were married?

Oh, that thought was forbidden. I was a lady of the mountain in training, and he was a traveling arena fighter. Nothing serious could ever come from this. Except that I was a romantic at heart, and I loved it when he told me stories about the north. I loved it when he was gentle with me. I loved...

"Oh," I breathed, shaking my head of dizzying thoughts and focusing on the now, "flushing toilets?"

"Unfortunately," he confirmed and then grabbed my hand. He leaned forward and kissed it as if I was a true lady. "I promise I'll be back in your bed before morning."

Then he was off to do the duties assigned to him, and I found myself with a free evening, something that rarely happened since I arrived at Elevar.

My prediction for the evening was that I'd finally start reading one of the books I borrowed from the shelf in the grand entrance. Kameron had suggested one that he said a good friend of his wrote. The way he said it with pride made me happy for him. It made me want to read the book and gush to him about it. That was until I went to the bathroom and discovered that the cold wet in my dress was blood and not just snow.

"Dead Gods," I grumbled, searching my skirts to see how much had been ruined by my moon blood and then getting dizzy when I realized the extent of it. "Why didn't Kameron say anything?" I grumbled to myself.

There was going to be no saving this gown, and belatedly I realized I hadn't bleed since before the Bloodstar died. I had nothing here to get me through a bleed, and my mind was strangely numb at trying to count the days. Four weeks after the Bloodstar died, or was it five? I hadn't had a bleed for three weeks before then. Why was it so late? And why was there so much!

Those questions might have made me panicky and weak if I didn't realize the question of "why" needed to wait for later. Right now, I required rags, a new gown, and probably some sleep to stave off nightmares. Gathering my dress up between my legs, I sighed and hoped that Ava was in the kitchen where she usually liked to be between clients. She had a knack for cooking up the most delicious meals.

Now that I was bleeding freely, I could feel it, heavier than any moonblood I ever experienced. My insides were twisting and turning, and the butterflies I thought I felt in my stomach when I was training with Kameron turned into cramps.

My discomfort must have been evident on my face when I got to the kitchen and found Ava and Kameron talking. They both turned to me, ceasing their conversation.

"Ava, I- I need help." I stumbled over my words and tried to stand up tall, but my insides protested. The older woman stepped towards me immediately.

"Oh, Lenora, let down your dress. Let me see how bad it is."

I hesitated to look at Kameron. For a second, I worried about him seeing the blood and then decided that was stupid. He was an arena fighter. His whole career was based in blood.

I did what Ava told me to, blanching at the feeling of unrestrained blood flowing down my thighs. Why was it so much? I wondered again before looking up to see Ava looking horrified and Kameron staring at me as if he would pass out. So much for handling blood well.

"When did you start bleeding?" Ava's voice wobbled.

"I don't know," It was hard not to gather my dress up again and press it to me, "Sometime between when I was outside with Kameron and now."

"You weren't bleeding when we were together." Kameron supplied, and that made me dizzy. I shouldn't be bleeding this much.

"Kameron, run. Fetch a doctor." Ava commanded. One second I saw Kameron, and the next, he was gone, not even a blur in my vision. I wondered how long it would take him to gather a doctor, but Ava pulled my attention back. She came over and grabbed me up by my arm, hoisting me forward. "Come on, Lenora. Let's get you to your room. Maybe laying down will help."

I walked along with her silently, laid down in my bed when she told me to, and fell asleep waiting for Kameron to return with a doctor.

Chapter Thirteen

"THAT CONTRACT IS UNFAIR!" Kameron bellowed when he heard the news. I cringed propped up in my bed, sipping on the medicinal tea prescribed to me. The teas helped with the bleeding, and all the girls said that the doctor probably saved my life. I didn't know. I couldn't remember what the doctor did to help me. It was a haze of swirls in my mind, like watching ocean waves crashing over and over and over again. I only heard from Ava that the procedure to cure me of bleeding had been intense. I ignored the doctor's words saying that this kind of bleeding happened when women failed to carry a child.

I was sure it was due to that. I was convinced that the beginnings of a new life had failed to take hold in me and was intensely relieved that they had. I didn't want Lukas's baby, not after he turned on me and blamed me for everything. I was sure I said that during the procedure, too, because whatever herbs they gave me to be still and complacent through it made me remember watching the waves come in—watching the houses crumble like sand against them—watching Mama drift out to sea. And the sea was blood, the blood of my body. The pain had been unbearable. And through the whole thing, I was told Kameron stayed by my side. He was by my side, now ranting and raving because I had to pay for the medical care given.

"I've been living here for a month without paying for anything, Kameron. Please calm down. I understand why Ava wants me to be responsible for the fee." I tried to speak softly so that he would stop pacing my room. So that he would think about it rationally.

I hoped it worked when he came to my bedside. But all I saw was the worried wrinkle of his forehead and the slight frown on his dark lips. Those lips I wanted to kiss but felt too faint to lean forward and do so.

"I can bargain for you, Lenora." He offered in a severe tone, "The rate that Ava wants of you will see you working for her forever. Client after client. Man after man. We already know you aren't made for that."

I swallowed a harsh mouthful of stinking tea and knew what he said was true—dreadful, genuine, and anxiety-producing.

"I don't like it either, but I don't know that I have any other option," I whispered. "Even if you bargain for me, I'll probably still have years of service. Dead Gods, I don't know why I ever thought I could somehow escape this."

Kameron yanked me towards him gently, pulling me into his arms and kissing my forehead. It felt good to have him by my side, but I realized with a lump in my throat that he would have to leave at some point. He had money to make too.

He had battles to win and places to be. Suddenly, I found myself wondering little things. Where did he live? What was his life like when he wasn't traveling from Arena to Arena?

Slowly I looked up to his deep eyes and let my lips move, "Kameron?"

"Yes?" I loved the deep tone of his voice. I wondered if anyone had loved him before.

"Why are you so worried about me?" Those weren't the words I was expecting to say, and I stumbled over myself, "I mean… you are worried about slavery, and it can't happen. It's illegal."

He blinked slowly and then laughed bitterly.

"I know you are naive, Lenora, but I didn't think you were that naive." Bristling in self-defense, I would have said something, but he went on. "I have a daughter in Davonne. She and her children are all enslaved. It's an old rule to get around the legality of it. They are responsible for the money that they would have made their miner masters had they been traditionally owned. Walking away from it carries a death penalty, and every new child born is calculated into the pool of what 'could have been earned'."

Horrified, I shook my head, "I had no idea." I didn't, for any of it. Kameron looked older than me, and logically I knew he had to be. Demons were long-lived and remained youthful for a very long time. And he had the slight look of crow's feet around his eyes, a bit of an everlasting wrinkle when he smiled. He must have been very old indeed.

"Why would you?" He responded with a short laugh. "I fight in the Arena's because the money I earn there goes back to my family and buys the freedom of another soul."

I had my answer. Kameron just traveled and fought, traveled and fought, over and over again to save his family from a fate he was watching me stumble my way into.

Biting my lip, I let him smooth his hands down my sides, comforting, soft. And my first question wouldn't leave me. Why me? Why be worried about me? Indeed, all the girls at Elevar had their debts to Ava? The older woman did charge me for new bedsheets, rags for bleeding, and the dress I ruined.

Even if the other girls knew medicines to stop bleeding from happening, Ava was supplying it, and that was probably a fee.

"Kameron?"

He grabbed my empty teacup putting it on the bedside table so that it wasn't between us. I didn't mind that his hand was wandering, up to my leg, over my stomach. He gently grasped my sore breast, massaging it with his strong hand.

"Yes?" I loved the way his voice rumbled and knew he was thinking about sex. Sex that we couldn't have because the doctor ordered abstinence for two weeks. But maybe I could do something for him. His other training came to mind.

I leaned over and caught his lips with mine—a soft kiss.

"You're so nice to me. I don't feel like I deserve it." I whispered and cut him off when he opened his mouth to tell me whatever reason he felt I did. "You make me want to support you, as much as you've supported me. But I own nothing; I have no power."

"You know how to punch now." He joked with a wild grin.

"And I'd love to continue our training and learn more fighting techniques from you, but you have places to be, don't you?" I think he got distracted because I put my hand on his chest and had him lean back against my pillows. The shadows in his eyes got darker, warmer somehow.

"Not at the moment. It will take a while for any of the Arena's to open up after the Bloodstar event. You've already told me there's a change in leadership for the Lopuri one, so I would expect they are probably not having a season, and it's too early to travel to Batomi Vidda." He said the words breathlessly as I unbuttoned his pants. "What are you doing?"

He didn't stop me. He lifted his hips to shimmy the pants down to his thighs. His cock sprang from the material, half-hard, beautiful. I flushed at what I was about to do.

"Uh... well... I figured I could still please you," I stuttered out, "You taught me what to do on my moon blood, and this isn't that much different from that." I had both hands around his cock, stroking softly up and down. Making him harder, making me heady and wanting even though this wasn't my time.

"Lenora," he moaned out my name and tossed his head back, all those beautiful braids splaying on my pillow. He was so into it already, and I loved that. Carefully I leaned over and licked the tip of his cock with my tongue. He moaned louder. Another lick, then another, until I was sliding my tongue back and forth across his slit while rubbing with my hands. I kept going, wanting his moans, wanting him to feel for me the way I felt for him. Eventually, I got a little more adventurous, taking the whole head of his cock into my mouth, marveling at the soft feel of it against my tongue. Sliding, slipping, wet.

Kameron strung his hands in my hair, whispering to me.

"Yes, Lenora... oh. You are such a good girl." Excited by his words, my whole body tingling, I tried to take more of him. Instantly I could tell it was the right move, the sliding motion, up and down with my whole mouth, causing him to groan breathlessly.

I wanted so very bad to make him cum. So bad that it filled up a fire in my gut and made me think I would orgasm if I ever got to see him cum. I knew it. It was so much of a truth that I moaned and discovered that the sound caused Kameron to thrust up. I tested it again, and before I knew it, he was thrusting in and out of my mouth at a languid pace.

"I'm gonna cum." He gasped a moment later, igniting a fire in my blood. I wanted this. I waited for this. "Ohhh..." He moaned, "Do you want it in your mouth?"

I loved that he thought to ask rather than just painting my face with it.

"Yes," my voice was breathy and ready, and I opened my mouth to take his head one last time. His cum shot into my mouth, tangy and salty. Keeping my mouth on his cock I swallowed as much as I could, listening to the contented groan he produced.

Slowly I sat back up, wiping away the little bits that had drizzled down my chin, and realized that despite my prediction, I hadn't cum myself, and I was ok with that. Bliss was still coursing through my veins, and I felt loved and proud of the way he looked at me and pulled me into his arms.

It was so warm surrounded by him. So good and perfect.

"I don't want this ever to end."

Those words slipped out of my mouth instead of staying in my head, and for a moment, I feared he'd react badly to them. But he just held me tighter and whispered in my ear.

"Let me possess you."

And you know what I said to the demon? Without a thought, without investigating why? Without understanding what this would mean for me? *Yes.*

"Yes," My voice sang stupidly, never once thinking that this would change everything.

Chapter Fourteen

PRESSURE EVERYWHERE, I COULD still feel his arms around me, but he was somehow under my skin, swirling around in my body and blood. Everything felt tighter. It was comforting for a second, breathtaking and delightful. Then I heard, without hearing a thing at all, because his voice was within me, a feeling of heat and ruffles inside my chest.

"I love this feeling," Kameron moved and didn't move at the same time. Shifting all of me to the left. Dizzying. "Are you alright, Lenora?"

"Yes..." I hesitated when my voice came out of my mouth. It felt weird to speak aloud to a person who was under my skin. I would have stayed in this comfortable spot, this sweet spot of existing together, but he took over my body without giving me a moment's respite.

My legs went numb first, then my fingers, the torpefying sensation crawling up my arms until I felt like I was floating inside myself, watching as my body moved to another's commands. My hands twitched, but all I could tell was a numb, barely-there reaction. Kameron lifted them, and it was much the same.

"You said you wanted to help me by doing this?" I reminded him, and he hummed in me, vibrating the core of me, shaking me up softly.

"I do. Sorry, it's been a long time since I've bonded with a partner this way. I almost forgot what it felt like." I would have responded to that, but he didn't let me. Instead, he looked through my memories as if they were magic that he could see. It let me see them too, detached, uninvolved from who I used to be.

He came upon the one that haunted me quickly. I saw myself walking down the road with Lukas and could feel the distant excitement that I felt for our sneaking off together.

Panicked, I started to watch the events of my past unfold before his eyes. The giggling naive girl I had been, the way Lukas steered me toward doom. We watched the passion together, which I thought was very one-sided from a critical eye and hindsight. We saw the moments when Papa and Mama found us. I felt Kameron flinch when my Papa hit me in the face. I felt his breath speed up in worry when we noticed the water.

Inside my body, he held me a little tighter as we sloshed our way out of the house. But then, when Mama helped me lift my dress to walk in the rising sea, the illusion of my memory cracked. My eyes, our eyes looked into Mama's face, and for a second, I saw her youthful, as young as me. I shook it off and realized it must be a memory of Kameron's before turning as I always did in this memory, away from her to the tree that would save me while she died.

Water water everywhere. I panicked again at the sight of it swirling up and up. Hyperventilating, I felt Kameron try to hug me with his soul, grounding me, reminding me that this wasn't real anymore. And while Mama died. My mind-numbed. I watched her float out to the sea again, blood in her face, no chances of making it away from the sea's terrible grip. Like in real life, I raged and cried and watched her form slide further from us. Away so far away, until all the water turned to dust. Everything around me evaporated, the landscape swirled and shook, and suddenly I was sitting very dry in the sunlight of a memory that wasn't my own.

"I'm going to marry him." It was my Mama's voice, reassured and healthy. My eyes let me look over to her, and a deep rumble came from my throat. Not my voice, though, not my memory.

"Go ahead. Why should I care?" Kameron spoke, and instantly I could tell he was lying, holding back. His chest was tight around us; his stomach churned into knots. He did care very much about what she was saying.

My Mama laughed and knelt wearing the leather raiment of the Arena's colors, nothing I had ever seen her in. She always wore dresses around me. But here, I could see her muscular legs, the strength in her arms, the slight indent of her waist.

"I'll see you inside then, hey Kam?" Mama said with a smile, "I'm going to beat you this time, just watch!"

She seemed utterly unaware of Kameron's eyes sizing her up, and just by the feelings dredged up in the demon's soul, I knew he wasn't sizing up an opponent. My heart tumbled out of my chest in the dark realization. He was sizing up a lover.

"I want out." My voice echoed in the expanse of him, in the hollowness of me. I didn't want to see this. I didn't want to know this. It spoiled things, made me feel weak, terribly taken. Was the only reason he liked me because he had once liked her? Kameron didn't respond. I watched him get up and brush the dirt off his roughspun pants. Then the world whooshed forward a moment until we were in a familiar place.

The Arena floor. The pale concrete floor had grates over the water pit and warped wood slats over those—the seats in the stadium that climbed up to the sky. The world was roaring around us, spectators screaming and singing.

Deep inside Kameron's mind, I could hear him chanting, "If I let her win, she'll have a better life. If I let her win, things will be harder for me. Either way, I'm going to lose her."

He looked over to the left, and I saw my Papa, young and scowling. He looked out over the Arena floor as if he was deeply upset by what he saw.

I was distraught too. I tried to reach out to Kameron again, but then our body zipped. We streaked fast past the world. He ran, and I lost my breath and senses. We came upon the left side of Mama standing there defenseless in the Arena. I think Kameron thought she was defenseless too because he got too close, and I don't know how she did it, listening to the wind maybe, but she lashed out.

I could tell she got a hit on Kameron. The memory of burning pain was deeply entrenched in his soul: pain and pride.

"I was the one who taught her how to fight." He explained to me when our body stuttered to a halt and stopped. "Just like I've been teaching you."

Kameron fell to the ground, and for the first time, I became aware of a dagger silver with strings of blood over it, poking out from his chest. I labored to breathe with him as one lung collapsed.

"Wh-why?" He asked when he looked up to see Mama's face looking down at him, "Paralyzing serum..." He mumbled incoherently, and I knew he was right. His arms and legs felt heavy, straining, struggling to stand, "I would have let you win. I love you."

I knew at that moment I was crying, trying to shake my head, trying to brush away the past. Kameron had loved Mama. I couldn't get over it, and then I couldn't believe the words I heard out of her mouth as the memory started getting fuzzy.

Kameron's vision started failing. Everything around us trickled to grey then black. But before me was Mama's face, hushing him.

"I don't believe you would have let me win. You are The Undefeated; a girl like me isn't going to change your mindset. Now go away, Kameron. I am in love with someone else. You could never have me."

I gasped and gurgled for breath and slowly felt all my limbs realign. Slowly felt as if I was alone inside my own body again. Staring at the ceiling of my room, I felt it when Kameron pulled his arms away from me.

"You weren't supposed to see those things." Silence followed his words. My heart was beating fast with anxiety. Crunching and curling through my chest, I opened my mouth to speak, and for a moment, no words came out, nothing but a pained moan. My throat felt sore, my mouth dry, but I had to know.

"Did you have me because I'm her daughter?"

Another long horrible silence followed.

"At first, yes." He confessed, "I knew the moment you told me that your mother was Julia the Brave that I wasn't going to pass up this opportunity. You look so much like her, and maybe I shouldn't have, but part of me wanted to pretend that I had gotten a chance to be with her."

I sobbed at those words. The horridness of them slamming down into my heart. Kameron didn't like me. He wanted me because he had a crush on my mother so very long ago. And she said no to him, she married my Papa, and he was the jealous one. And I am the jealous one. Both of us existed in pain.

"I won't lie to you, Lenora," Kameron said, "It started that way, but I quickly knew you were your own person. And I grew to want you for who you are. I want to save you. I want to be with you."

Each word felt like a dagger laced with petrification poison, just like the one that brought him down in the Arena. My head hurt, my body hurt. Emotionally I was a tattered mess wringing my hands into the bedsheets and sobbing over his words.

I had let this demon into my heart. I allowed Kameron to possess me. And I couldn't help but wonder if the only reason he did it was to have one last look at her.

"Go..." I gasped.

"Lenora?"

"Go. I don't want to see you again."

My bed shifted. I felt his weight slide off, but I still couldn't look at him through my salty tears.

"I'm sorry." He whispered before leaving my room and letting me wallow in the hurt that burned inside my heart.

Chapter Fifteen

THE GRAVITY DIDN'T HIT me until two days later when Ava dragged me out of bed and told me it was my turn to flush the toilets. No matter that, I was still bleeding. No matter that, I was sick unto myself for everything that happened.

It didn't matter that I missed Kameron immediately. My skin felt cold without him, and my days were empty.

"You cost us good money," Ava huffed at me, yanking my wool dress over my head, "Kameron pays good money, and you sent him away! What in the name of the Dead Gods were you thinking?"

"Sorry," I said without being sorry to her at all. Everything was numb and dull, and she cursed me some more before tugging me down the hall and to the main door.

"For your stupidity, you'll be doing toilet duty for the next week." She scowled, "The first lesson you should have learned was always to make the client happy, no matter what."

I nodded to her as complacent as I could while my heart bled inside. She was right. I was stupid to send Kameron away. What I should have done was ask for some space to think about this. Maybe ask that he sleep with Anni that night.

Filling up my buckets with packed snow, I couldn't help but cry. Out here in the sunshine of the tiny valley where Elevar sat. Mountain birds chirping in the evergreens, and the bray of goats that we kept for milk and food filled my ears. Over that, all was the sound of my sobs. Regret, pain, needing to know more, needing to believe him.

"Stop crying so loudly!"

At first, I thought Ava was coming out to scold me again, but when I wiped my tears with my wet mittens, I saw Anni kneeling by my side. Her long black hair reached the snow spreading out like fractals of black against the white. They reminded me of Kameron's marks, and it made me sniffle again.

"No, don't cry. Ava doesn't know I'm out here." Anni whispered, "Look, Kameron told me what happened."

"I made a mistake." I sniffled, "I shouldn't have told him to go. I should have believed him. It was just so…"

"Overwhelming? Yes, sometimes demonic possession makes people react stronger to things than they normally would have." Ava said as soothingly as she was able to.

"H-have you ever been possessed?"

"No, but I've read about it in old texts from the Rathinian Empire. Even among modern demons, it is not a strong practice. You have to understand that Kameron is very, very old." Anni grabbed my hands, "Kameron told me that he had hoped that the experience would bring you both closer together."

I felt cheated in those moments because I wasn't sure that it did. I sent Kameron away stupidly, and I still had questions, still had feelings about what I learned.

"I want him back," I confessed as quietly as I could as if the gods would hear me if I spoke any louder. "I love him." Anni just smiled at me and patted my hands. The wet mittens were cold against my fingers, and I knew what I had to do. "I have to run away from Elevar," I whispered.

"I'll try to give you a few hours head start. But you do owe Ava quite a bit of money when you see Kameron remind him of that. Maybe he can cover the costs you accrued."

"And what about you?" I asked.

"This is my home, darling. I'm never leaving." Anni laughed softly, "But it will be lonely not having Kameron come around anymore. I'll be sad to see you leave too."

I didn't know if it could comfort her or not, but I leaned over and hugged her tightly.

"We will come back for you." Anni didn't acknowledge my whispered words as I stood up and looked towards the pass that led to Lopuri.

Homeward. It was going to be an arduous journey by myself, but I had to do it. I had to find Kameron and let him know he meant the world to me, despite my conflicted feelings.

.

Chapter Sixteen

"YOU SHOULDN'T BE HERE, Lenora." My brother's words were harsh but not as painful as the sores on my feet from having walked over a week from Elevar to Lopuri. Miles of walking down the old mountain pass, snow in my shoes, no cart to carry me. When I went with Papa and Mateo, we at least had a coach up to Amapola before making the trek on foot. I clenched my fists, looking up to his impassioned face.

"I just need to know if The Undefeated is here."

All I was after, just him. I hoped my brother would give me the information and then let me leave. I'd never see him again if he wanted, but I needed to find Kameron. I needed to tell him the truth; that I loved him, that the things in our past didn't matter, that I was a fool for telling him to go.

"I haven't seen the monster. Why would you even be looking for The Undefeated?" Jonathan asked, but I was no longer interested in answering his questions. I frowned and wondered how I was going to find Kameron in such a big city. When he said he was coming here, I had assumed that it was for the Arena, but I didn't know where else he would have or could have gone.

"Do you know where he stays when he's not at the Arena?" I demanded to know, all while sneaking around his question.

His face, so much like our Papa's, just looked at me with perplexed disgust. I didn't know that I could get anything more out of him, which meant I needed to find another source of information. I turned on my heels looking out over Lopuri, wondering where I could go. Where could Kameron have gone?

Jonathan grabbed my arm roughly. My brother spun me around, fingers digging in.

"You didn't answer me. Why are you looking for The Undefeated? You're supposed to be with Papa and Auntie and Uncle. How did you get back here?"

An uncomfortable tightness filled my throat at that. Was it safe to tell him? Probably not, but I didn't know what other lie I could come up with.

"Papa abandoned me." I hesitated to tell him where "I'm looking for Kameron because he's helped me stay alive. I have a debt to repay him."

It seemed to be good enough. Jonathan frowned and let me go. Crossing his big arms in front of his chest, he wiggled his jaw from side to side. I missed seeing him think, I realized. I felt the loss of my family deep in my heart. Even if he wasn't happy to see me, I was determined to count this as a blessing. After a moment, he grunted.

"If The Undefeated is in Lopuri, he's probably staying at the hostel where most of our traveling fighters stay." Untangling his arms, he pointed down the road towards the beachside part of the city. "It's called Clementina's Resort and is right on the north side of the shore by the boardwalk."

"Thank you so much, Jonathan." I gushed, "If I could make it up to you?"

"Just stay safe, Lenora. It's not the best area of town. Lots of beggars, lots of men who might try to take advantage of you." I didn't ask why he wasn't going to accompany me. I figured he was still angry with me, still blaming me for Mama's death. He wasn't wrong, I was responsible through the stupid choices I made, and it still hurt to see him put distance between us. As if we weren't siblings, as if we weren't family.

I took a deep breath in, thanked him again, and then walked down to the beachside, down many twisty roads, between whitewashed houses. Things in this area of town looked like they hadn't been affected at all by the Bloodstar's death.

The flowers for the dry season were starting to bloom, crimson, gold. I kept to myself walking down to the open boardwalk. It was quiet in midmorning, the restaurants not yet open for the day, though a few older ladies were selling seared scallops out of their cart. My stomach rumbled. The last time I ate was in Amapola after sneaking through the trash of their inn for scraps.

"This would have been a lot easier if I grabbed money before running away," I grumbled to myself and rushed past the food stalls, past the giant statue of a sea monster in the center of town.

I went down the north road, unsure of how I would recognize this hostel until I came to a spot where the stone seawall met the end of the road. There were men outside fighting, practicing. And as soon as they saw me, they began hollering, whistling, calling out like lusty youths who haven't any manners. Now, if Mama taught me anything about the Arena, the men who went there were this sort of wild bunch. I must be in the right spot.

"Is this Clementina's Resort?" I questioned, holding my head high.

"Sure is, sweetie," One of the men who was fighting in the front leered at me. He ran his hands down his sweaty arms and grinned, "What's a pretty girl like you doing down here?"

I would have answered honestly. I would have boldly proclaimed my search for The Undefeated when another familiar voice called out to me.

"Lenora?" Lukas called to me, coming out from inside the house as if he loved me and hadn't tried to blame Mama's death on me. He was grinning as he jogged up to me, as happy as I had ever seen him if not a bit unwashed and ungroomed. He held out his arms and exclaimed, "Oh, thank the gods you've come back to me! You wouldn't believe what I've suffered in your absence!"

I didn't care, and where I might have shrunk back in discomfort before, I felt strong now. Clenching my fists, I remembered Kameron's lessons. The right way to punch, the way to run if I needed to escape. When Lukas reached me, I lashed out, striking him right in the chest.

He went down, rough, scraping his knees into the roadway. Breathless.

"I'm not taking you back after what you said about me," I yelled at him. "You ungrateful jerk! I risked my reputation to have a relationship with you, and then you blamed me for my mother's death! Who does that?"

Lukas was still on the ground holding the spot where I hit. He gasped and wheezed, and it felt good to see him kneeling at my feet. It felt good that all these other men had stopped what they were doing to watch.

"How did you learn to punch like that?" He finally got out, not even acknowledging the rest of my words. Irritatingly not groveling and saying apologies I felt I deserved. How much he suffered since the Bloodstar died was nothing compared to what I experienced. I was sure he hadn't almost died from blood loss because of our one time together.

Sneering down to him, I tried to look like a poised figure, "Kameron Marks taught me how to fight." I boasted.

That got the men watching us talking, whispering among themselves. I didn't know what they said, and I hoped whatever it was commanded respect for me because even though I could land a punch on Lukas, there was no way I could take them all on.

"The Undefeated taught you how to punch?" Lukas finally stood up, still hunched over. He grumbled, "I'd believe it. What the hell are you doing here then? Decided to follow Mama's footsteps and become a fighter?"

Chin high. Chin high, I reminded myself before speaking, "I am here for Kameron. That is all. Where is he?"

"He went up to the Castillo House." One young man called out. "A woman with no skin came and got him."

"A woman with no skin?" I shuddered and glanced past the hostel up the long hill of the peninsula to the Castillo House. I could see the old tower in the distance, but not much else of it, and groaned. "Is he coming back?" I called out, wishing that he would so that I could take a break from walking, especially walking uphill.

"I don't know, girl! I don't keep tabs on The Undefeated. The man's insane."

I didn't think he was, but I knew that he could be intimidating. I knew because he told me that most fighters fought with persona's, and The Undefeated was a snarky malicious sort of fighter, whereas typically Kameron was relatively calm. Of course, it probably came off as insanity to other combatants.

Turning around, I tried to remember what roads would lead up to the Castillo House, stomach growling, mind fuzzy.

"I need to get to him fast," I grumbled more to myself than anyone else. My limbs were prickling with the pain of having stood too long, and for a moment, I feared dropping right in front of the hostel and these men I didn't know I could trust.

I put one foot in front of the other and walked, hoping beyond hope that the Castillo House was my final destination.

Chapter Seventeen

WHEN I FINALLY GOT to the Castillo House, it was night. The darkness had fallen all around and cooled the constantly humid, always hot air of the city. I stood outside on the painted road up to the Castillo House, surrounded by walls of beautiful murals. Reds and blues, painted shells, and sea-washed stones made beautiful patterns all around me, but I wasn't there for the sights. I wasn't a tourist like so many on the road. Instead, I was utterly unable to get into the gated entrance of the Castillo House, where you needed passes and permission to access the halls of diplomats and lawmakers, of Princes and Kings.

"I'm sorry, miss, but you don't have papers you don't get in." One of the guards was saying to me dutifully, his orange sash pinned smartly to his shoulder. My empty hands trembled, and my mind raced. I looked dirty and road-weary, and I knew it. There was no reason this man should comply with my request.

"I know, but…" I tried again, breathing in, breathing out a prayer with my words.

"No papers, no entry." He repeated. That seemed to be final. The guard turned away from me and went to his post— the whole of the Castillo House off-limits to me.

I felt like I could collapse into the roadway in hunger and exhaustion. Frustration gnawed at me even further, and I thought, *there has to be another way*. Another way to get to Kameron and the skinless woman. I shuddered. What would he be doing with someone from the Castillo House anyway?

Plodding along, I went to a side street off the painted road, following the old stone wall of the Castillo House, looking up every so often for an opportunity. Fearfully I thought it wouldn't present itself because the further down the road I went, the taller the wall rose in the background of houses. Still, it came just as the road sloped down. Behind one of the houses was a section of the Castillo's wall that had crumbled. It was just enough that the wall was probably climbable. I rallied myself up to the idea of trespassing on the private property of whoever's house this was, and on the grounds of King Martin!

Did I dare do such a thing?

I only hesitated a moment because it seemed silly that I wouldn't dare. I ran away from a sizable debt in Elevar, let a demon possess me, fought men who could have killed me, and had an illicit relationship with my adopted brother that caused my life to turn upside down.

Of course, I was going to climb the wall to find love.

If my body didn't give in first.

Wobbling, I walked into the yard of the house as quietly as I could, I put my hands on the falling stones of the wall, and

I pulled myself up. Every muscle was protesting as I started my ascent. Even broken, the wall was twice as tall as I was.

"Uhg..." I moaned in pain and then berated myself for letting out a sound. The wall was harder to climb than I expected, even from the broken parts. I struggled, and then when I finally had my legs over the side, I got dizzy looking down. Biting my lip, I sat there in the twilight around Lopuri for some long moments. *This is going to hurt.* The dreadful drop was even lower on the side of the Castillo House, and there was nothing there to cushion a fall. My breath sped up in a panic, but I couldn't do anything but let myself drop down into a flower bed along a path.

The ground hit me hard, faster than I would have liked. Bone crunching, vomit-inducing. I could see the tunnel of unconsciousness hit me, making all my vision narrow into a tiny circle before the black.

And in the black, I stayed, quiet, still. I was slowly becoming aware of light and warmth and his voice. I woke up to Kameron speaking.

"I swear to you, Goddess, I will protect her."

The light came back slowly, and I made the realization that I was nowhere near where I had fallen. I was inside a room with a stone ceiling and wooden beams laid across it to hold it up, under warm blankets and the scent of a savory broth nearby. My stomach ached for food, but I shifted to see if I could find Kameron in the room. My eyes searching, I caught sight of him in front of a doorway blocking a bright light. A light that seemed unreal. *A God.*

I gaped for a second before the pain in my legs became too much and caused me to moan out. I saw the light disappear, and Kameron turned around quickly. His dark eyes scanned over me as he rushed forward to the bedside.

"Lenora, thank goodness you are awake!" His big hands held onto my shoulders, and I felt a sharp pain in the left one that made me wince.

"Ah! That hurt!" I gasped out.

"Yes, you have several broken bones from falling off the wall," Kameron muttered. "Why did you do it? It was so dangerous. You could have died!" His frantic words just made me smile.

"I did it for you. To get to you." I took a deep breath in, "I was wrong to send you away. I'm sorry." I looked into his eyes, so full of love and acceptance. I knew that with him was where I wanted to be.

He was silent for a few minutes, and I hoped that he'd accept my apology because if he didn't, I didn't know what would become of my life. I risked everything I had left for him. But it wasn't him who spoke next. It was a voice familiar and numbing, someone I had never expected to hear again.

"My little Lenora, didn't I tell you the Arena was bad news?" Mama's voice parted through the room, commanding and ethereal, and when she came up to Kameron's side, I understood. She had no skin, just blisters and blood that glowed like the stars. All of her pretty brown hair that I envied as a child was gone. But her eyes were the same, the mismatch of color, the smile lines around the lids.

"Ma-Mama!" I cried, horrified by Mama's condition and elated by her escape from death. I knew, with a jolt to my heart, that the goddess Kameron had been talking with was her. I had no idea how or what made gods, but it was unmistakable to look upon one. It was stunning.

"Yes, Lenora, hush. Kameron's told me... enough." She whispered diplomatically, "Now it's obvious you've run away from Elevar with a substantial debt to the organization."

My stomach churned for a moment, and I worried she'd send me back. Kameron just kept petting down my shaking fingers.

"I don't want to go back, Mama."

"I don't want you there. That is no place for my daughter, and I curse your father for bringing you there." She paused, and I felt terrible that I was still horrified by the look of Mama's skin. This was my mother, uplifting and supporting me, and all I could see was blistered skin and blood so bright it rivaled stars. I wondered if she'd ever look normal again.

"Don't be scared," Kameron whispered, holding my fingers tight, "Julia's the same person she was before becoming a goddess. The same mother you knew."

"Alright," My teeth chattered anyway. There was a shake of my limbs that I could not control.

"I will pay off your debt and set you free," Mama whispered and leaned forward. I tried not to flinch when she patted my hair down. "I trust Kameron to take care of you after that."

"But you always said the Undefeatable was a horrible person." I mumbled even though I knew in my heart, he wasn't, "Why? And why are you two together now?"

They looked at each other then back at me. Mama straightened up.

"Your father told me he was horrible, that he was planning on selling me to Elevar as soon as we traveled north to Diss. I believed the wrong person." Mama said curtly. "I am sorry that he did that to you."

Then Kameron cleared his throat.

"I heard word that your mother survived her time out to sea and was suffering in her first days as a Goddess. I came to the Castillo House to tell her what I know about the changing of mortals into gods and how she could make things easier on herself." Kameron explained, "You were not wrong, Lenora; I loved your mother. I still do, but not the way you think." As soon as he was done speaking, he leaned forward and kissed me, lips sliding over mine, deep, passionate pressure. He didn't ask this time when he slipped into my body—possessing me the way that his kind could, soul pressed against my soul. The heat and wonder of him filling me up with delight. It was momentary bliss before he let go. I was dizzy again, almost faint when he pulled back.

I flushed in embarrassment and glanced back at Mama. She was simply standing and watching us. Calm and serene despite her appearance. She didn't seem to care about my relationship with Kameron, and for that, I was thankful and humbled.

"Kameron, you will marry my daughter; make a proper woman out of her," Mama demanded. Kameron met her no-nonsense tone with a laugh.

"If you will have me, Lenora." His voice smoothed over me. "I'm afraid I don't have a proper home in the city, and I've married many times before."

"Yes," I choked out, "I don't care about all that. I simply want you." I was so glad when he kissed me again and began to imagine my future for real. I was not the secret lover of my brother or a woman trapped in Elevar. My destiny was being the wife of Kameron Marks, The Undefeated, traveling with him throughout the world.

I could never have imagined anything better.

Chapter Eighteen

"AARON! NO! YOU DUMBASS! What are you doing out there?"

I chuckled at Kameron's exasperated yelling and shifted foot to foot in the Arena's side rooms. In my arms, our daughter, Valerie, looked in awe at her father.

"Mama," She asked, turning her pretty face towards me. I noted that I should redo her braids before we started traveling. Keep the snarls away. "Why is Daddy so loud?" She complained. Her cute chubby cheeks turned down into a frown, and I had to laugh.

"He's just having fun, Val." I brushed my nose against her's. From out in front of us, the familiar, exuberant cheers of the Arena filled the air. I paused, waiting for them to die down, "And you're going to have fun here too. First, we are going to the Diss arena to watch Daddy fight, then Moorelend, then Lopuri, where we will visit Grandma..."

"But Grandma is here?" Valerie questioned, pointing out to me what I already knew. I laughed softly.

"Yes, Grandma is visiting us right now, but she has to go back to her home, and that is in Lopuri. So don't you worry, Val, by the time we get there, Grandma will be waiting for us."

"But why?"

I sighed; it was neverending with four-year-olds.

I didn't bother trying to explain how traveling over the empire worked or that grandma didn't live with us here in Batomi Vidda. She just visited when we were home and not making the rounds from arena to arena, city to city. Instead, I waited for Kameron to come back to us away from the open cages surrounding this arena. He did eventually shake his head and curse the new guy.

"I don't know why I bother to train new fighters," Kameron winked at me. "They are all trouble, either turning their backs on their opponents or stealing my heart."

"Stealing your heart?" I teased, "Is that what you call it? I thought I was just keeping your house for you."

Leaning in, he kissed me hard, lips pressed against mine, tongue shoved in my mouth, and when we tried to pull apart, our sweet little girl smooshed our faces together again.

"Kiss! Kiss!" she chanted in her tiny little voice.

"Now, Val!" Kameron grabbed her up from my arms as we started to walk out of the Arena. No one bothered us along our path. A few men called out a goodbye, but in this, the roughest of the empire's arena's, we were just part of the family. "How would you like to get some jad before we go home for the night? It's the last time we will be able to get sweet jad for a long time."

"Why?" Valerie asked, ever curious. Kameron sighed and turned to me.

"She still doesn't understand that we are traveling tomorrow?"

"No, but she'll get it. You have to remember, Kam, I haven't been on the journey since she was born. Val doesn't know any of it."

"That's probably true," He mused and then distracted us by playing a game with our little girl. We spent the evening eating jad covered in sugar and spices and running around the yard of our tiny city home. When it came time for bed, Mama came and took little Val and let Kameron and I continue packing for our journey.

Before I got pregnant with Valerie, we would rent a carriage and backpack the whole journey. I've met his family in Davonne, and we spent so much time laughing and journeying, and now it was time to bring our little girl on the trip with us.

"I'm excited we got a ship this time," I gushed while folding some of his clothes for our trunk.

"Yes, I know. I remember you saying so." Kameron laughed right behind me. I glanced back just in time for him to circle his arms around me. He pressed his body up against mine, and I giggled.

"Mama didn't take Valerie so that we could have sex." I scolded, teasingly, soft. "We're supposed to be packing."

We were supposed to be packing, but that wasn't what was going to happen. Kameron spun me around quickly, hands clasped over my wrists pulling my arms up. Greedy lips on mine, his breath was my life.

"I want you badly," He grumbled in my ear, guiding my hand down to his lap. I could feel his cock through his pants, thick, big, ready.

"You have me every day," I giggled but smoothed my fingers down the bulge anyway. "Insatiable ass."

"Can't help it that you're so beautiful." His fingers worked at the button of his pants, quickly popping it open, dropping the material to the floor. I knelt with it, licking his cock from base to head, enjoying the way he shivered under my touch. I enjoyed the way his demon marks lit up and the way he gathered his breath expectantly. Then I devoured him. My mouth was sliding over his cock, taking in as much as I could, wanting, needing to show him that I enjoyed this activity as much as he did.

He moaned and strung his fingers through my hair, pulling my head back gently.

I let him lift me to the bed. I shivered when he took the time to unbutton my dress, to take my breasts in his mouth as he uncovered them. His fingers slid down my skin, up my thighs. I was shivering when he gently caressed over my knees and dove back down. My lily was open to him, ready and waiting, and his fingers danced over my skin.

I moaned.

"What do you want?" Kameron growled in my ear. His tongue lapped against my earlobe. His fingers kept sliding over my wet flesh. I gasped and flushed, needing him to go faster, to fulfill me. Hot, ready.

"L-lick me." I stuttered out, "I want you to make me cum."

Magic words. He chuckled and then moved down his tongue trailing wet lines over my skin, across the peaks of my breasts, down into my belly, and then finally to my lily. His tongue pressed flat against my petals, smoothed up and over the bud, and made me wiggle.

"More!" I cried. He went slow again, teasing me, raising the heat, slow, sensual. I thought I might die if he kept this pace, so close to lightning striking so close to completion. "Please, Kameron, go faster!" I pressed my hips up to his face, gently, not enough to unseat him, but enough to get a fraction more pressure, a fraction more indulgence.

I thought I heard him laugh before he dove in, licking hard and robust up, wiggling his tongue over my bud. He was pulling me close and closer. He added a finger, slipped it into me, and then another one pumping me as he sucked away, and all the burning heat in me lifted to a crescendo. Thighs tightened up, my stomach spasmed, and I came moaning so loud that probably the whole house could hear me, but I didn't care.

I only cared that I was here, with the man I loved. Kameron mounted me quickly, and I could feel the urgency under his skin as I dizzily came down from my high. His cock pounded into me steady, strong, fast. I was so tender that minor aftershocks kept me on my toes, stretched for him and his big cock.

"Harder." I gasped, and he complied, angling deeper, pushing rougher. His breath started to sound ragged. "Cum in me."

"I will." He groaned. "I'm there." His voice broke, and suddenly he was pressing as deep as he could cock twitching inside me. I moaned again, loving the feeling, enjoying it with every fiber of my being.

We stayed frozen on the cusp of pleasure for a few moments before Kameron broke it by kissing my lips. He pulled out gently, and the wetness of our lovemaking slid all over me.

I sighed deeply, wrapping my arms around him on our bed, looking up to the spackled ceiling. A ceiling I wouldn't see again for almost a year.

"I love you, Kameron," I whispered.

"I love you too." He responded, again pressing a kiss to my lips. We fell asleep like that cuddling, just like we cuddled through all the cold nights.

ABOUT THE AUTHOR

Leah hails from the sandy beaches of Hawaii where she spends her days reading whatever she can get her hands on and playing maid to her small menagerie of animals. She's always preferred her stories to have a fun mix of playful and steamy, and likes getting right to the point. She writes in a variety of genres and pairings, hoping that each reader will find something they enjoy.

BOOKS BY THIS AUTHOR

Under B.G. Hing
Deliver Us From Evil Series
Bloodstar

Under Leah Hantel
Luring the Moon
Hunted
Miss Magic
The Demons I Love

Featured in Anthologies

Wings of Ash
Frosted: A Winter PNR Anthology

More to Come!